WICKED

GAME

a novel

Gerri Wilson

Cover by Dave Myers, Dave Myers Design 2015

Wicked Game a novel

Copyright @ 2012 by Gerri Wilson

www.wickedgameanovel.com

Published by Pinnacle SE Publishing, Inc. 2012, Hilton Head Island, SC 29928, www.pinnaclesepublishing.com

Printed in the United States of America.

Acknowledgements

To God, for the gift of imagination and the ability to write it down.

Jeff, without your love, support and encouragement...this project could have never materialized.

Pappy, you've always believed in me.

Contributing Editor: Jeffrey T. Wilson

"Known Terrorist Dead, President says" - USA Today

"Got Him" - New York Post

"Rot in Hell" - New York Times

"Justice has been Done" - Washington Post

"We got the Bastard" - Philadelphia Enquirer

"Terrorist Buried at Sea" - USA Today

"Killed"- Charlotte Observer-San Diego Tribune

"He's Dead" - Miami Herald

* * * * *

The headlines today, May 2, 2011, a remarkable feat accomplished. Finally, closure for a country suffering nearly 10 years from the worst disaster ever to take place on American soil.

"Good morning beautiful. You are so beautiful in the morning," he says as he rolls over to kiss his wife while turning on his iPad.

"Morning...coffee?" With a sweet peck on his cheek, she gently rolls out of her side of the bed.

"That would be great babe. Oh my God, look at these headlines!" he shouts. She leans over the bed and peeks over her husband's shoulder at the front page headlines of the New York Times on his iPad.

"What?" she exclaims.

"The Seals took him out last night. Where the hell were we?"

"In bed at 8 o'clock recuperating from my father's wedding Saturday night, remember? I am going to call him."

Throwing back the covers and jumping out of bed, he agrees. "Great idea. I can't wait to see what he has to say about this."

She grabs her robe, iPhone in her ear and heads for the kitchen to make coffee. "Hey, I hate to bother you but I can't believe it. What happened?" she says into the phone. On the other end of the line her father's voice, "I don't know the details other than what you have probably already seen this morning, but isn't it great news!"

"Dad, this is incredible, so many will finally have closure. What a great coup for the President."

"Yes it certainly is, sweetheart. A great day in America."

"I am going to get ready for work and let you get back to your honey moon, will you call me later?" "Of course sweetheart. You two have a great day. I will talk to you later."

"Okay Daddy, thanks, love you."

"Love to you two." Her father disconnects the call.

She finishes the coffee, iPhone still lodged between her shoulder and ear and heads back to the bedroom, a cup of joe in each hand.

Her husband is just getting out of the shower wrapping a towel around his very cut waist. "Did you reach your father?"

"Yes, isn't this incredible?" she says handing him a cup as she admiringly checks out her very handsome husband's physique. She is as enamored with him today as she was the first day they met in college at NYU over fifteen years ago.

* * * * *

THREE YEARS EARLIER

Three young friends clandestinely drawn into an international event of which they had no idea of the significance, will change their lives forever.

APRIL, 2008... It's a beautiful day just outside of Havana, Cuba, 80 degrees, not a cloud in the sky. The turquoise waters are glistening in the sunlight and the sounds of the surf and sea birds peacefully reign at this most luxurious paradise estate. On the veranda a man is playing cards alone with the beautiful blue water in the distance. A second man enters, tall, attractive, sporting a beautifully tailored suit. He walks out onto the veranda towards the other. They shake hands and are seated. A servant follows with a tray of cool drinks.

"Ah, the gatekeeper or should I say broker? What brings you to paradise today?" The second man hands him an envelope of documents which he opens, briefly reviews and returns them to the envelope, setting it beside him on his chair.

"I just wanted to personally inform you that everything is on schedule, all arrangements have been confirmed and we have less than 60 days to wait this out, and then...you are a free and admonished man. You should be very humbled that we were able to negotiate in this manner."

"Yes, it has worked out rather nicely for all of us though I do not completely trust the US government, of course. These documents will be proof enough of their ultimate stupidity, and will be used against them if necessary." The man looks away toward the sea.

"Of course that is true." says the second man. "It is quite a coup."

The other man sighs, "Yes, indeed, though the Americans I am sure are celebrating what they believe to be THEIR victorious coup," both men chuckle.

"I am happy that you are in agreement and understand the time line.   You have quite lovely surroundings here to enjoy until fruition." The second man reassures his captive guest.

"It will do," says the man, "I can have this anywhere in the world at any time, but I will play their game for now. Ultimately, it will be worth it, I suppose. It will ease my family of their grief and concern for my well being. I only do this for them."

"I will allow you to return to your card game," the second man with a pious half smile comments. "I will be in touch."

As the polished courier departs the room, the man never acknowledges his leaving and seemingly returns to his lonely game of cards. The posted guards escort the visitor to his waiting black sedan under the portico entrance and it exits through the gates of the estate.

HIGH ATOP A HILLSIDE, some distance away, a professional photographer is working, taking shots of this most scenic beach area. His very long zoom lens catches in a corner of the frame, the gentleman entering the car. His instinctive lens moves from this scenic image of turquoise water and beautiful blue skies to the distant image. The camera begins clicking furiously, almost as if it has taken over the actions of its photographer. As the man enters his shiny black car and exits the grounds of this most exquisite estate, a nearly blinding streak of light bounces from the sedan towards the lens, reflecting off the car from the bright sunlight, though the camera continues to follow.

As the car fades in the distance after leaving this exquisite and heavily guarded estate, the photographer casually returns to the matter at hand, almost as if he had never broken away from his task of filming the beautiful blue water and sugary sand beach.

* * * * *

TWO WEEKS LATER, it is a crisply bright and sunny day at Laguardia Airport. Inside the terminal, photographer Patric Taylor walks through the corridor carrying a large travel duffle, his face tan, beard rough, his black Tommy Bahama button down shirt, buttoned down exposing his tee shirt underneath tucked into his snug and low hugging Seven jeans. Patric Taylor is a magnetically attractive, 30 something, free-spirited looking man. When he walks, it is as if he is floating in slow motion.   His tall, svelte stature is even more endearing with the dark tan and dark Ray-Ban shades. He leaves the airport terminal and hails a cab.

"How are you doing?" Patric speaks to the driver, "Eighth Avenue between 40th and 41st."

"Okay, 8th Avenue," confirms the driver.

"The New York Times Building." Patric clarifies with the driver his exact destination.

"Yes, sir."

The New York City skyline is magnificent today as the cab crosses the bridge toward midtown.   The tall buildings reflect the gleaming sunlight in the forefront to a crystal clear and deep blue sky. Patric is glad to be back in the city and ready to get back to work. Reviewing new emails and text messages on his phone, it beeps with a new text message. It reads, "*Are you back on this side of the pond?*"

Patric responds typing, "*Yes, on my way to your office, see you shortly Bro.*" His best friend, Tim Connelly, NY Times writer, hires him as a free lance photographer on occasion and needs him today. They both love the opportunity to work together. As life gets in the way at times, the two old friends don't have the opportunity to spend time together as they did in the "old days" partying and carousing the city as young single guys, though Patric is still very much a bachelor.

The cab stops in front of the beautiful New York Times Building at 620 Eighth Avenue, the 52 story tower which was just completed and opened a year earlier in 2007. It had moved from its location on West 43rd Street, but stayed in the Times Square area which was named after the paper when the Times moved to 42nd Street in 1904. The Times owns the 2nd to 27th floors. Their partner in the building, Forest City Ratner Companies occupies floors 29-52 as well as some retail on the first floor. Other tenants in the building include law firms, Dean and DeLuca, the New Jersey Nets, various consulting firms, etc. Typical New York City skyscraper, except you won't find a medical office, employment agency or social service agency. They are prohibited in accordance with the terms of the original lease documents. Patric enters the building as the cab whizzes off, he proceeds up the elevator through a few rows of cubicles to the outside office of *Senior Staff Writer, Tim Connelly.*

"Welcome back…how were the Bahamas?"

"Great my friend. I actually took a flight over to Cuba for a couple of days to check it out."

"Really, how was that?" Tim remarks curiously. Tim and Patric couldn't be more opposite. Tim, the preppy, starched shirt, straight laced looking, studious writer and Patric, the free spirited, creative photographer, but for nearly 20 years, since their college days at NYU, the two were inseparable.

"Interesting architecture." There is a pause.

"Patty my boy, is that all you have to say about it? Are you talking buildings or women? Hey, speaking of great buildings, I ran into Rebecca Saturday night. She was with some tall dark foreign looking guy. She looks good man…you really screwed that up for yourself."

Patric rolls his eyes, "Yeah, whatever…so, who was the dude?"

"She said he was a client. You still have it bad for her don't you?"

"I just asked who the dude was. Bec and I settled our deal a long time ago. I don't have it in me to be an old married guy like you my friend. How is your beautiful wife doing anyway?" Patric tries to change the subject and his efforts are successful.

"She's feeling good, starting to look a little like a linebacker though. I'll be glad when the kid gets here and she can stop worrying so much about her tummy. I'm kind of diggin' the Ta Ta's though. Are you ready to get to work? We have a train to catch to DC to hit a press conference this evening. The VP is going to make a statement about Guantanamo. Should be right up your alley since you are now a Cuba expert."

"When did you become the DC desk, TC?"

"Since I am the senior staff writer and political expert here at the Times...a n d since my counterpart in DC had emergency back surgery last week and is off the desk for six weeks. You should feel honored, I maneuvered you in as my personal camera man, plus I thought it would be cool for us to have a night on the town in DC...like the old days. We'll head back in the morning." Looking at Patric's duffle, "I see you are already packed."

"Not for DC, Mr. Senior Staff Writer, but I can make it work. Okay, let's do it!" Up to the task, and looking forward to some guy time with his pal, Patric is all in.

Tim grabs his sport coat from the back of his chair throwing it over his shoulder and picks up his brief case and overnight bag from behind the desk. As the two leave the office Tim takes a good look at his friend and partner. "Can ya just button up the shirt ole' buddy?" They both laugh and make their way to the elevator.

* * * * *

DOWNTOWN IN A BEAUTIFUL OFFICE, overlooking the Hudson, a striking young woman sits at her desk taking in the breathtaking view, somewhat deep in thought. As her office phone rings, she sighs and answers, "Rebecca Webb."

"Hello," a man's voice responds.

"Hello to you...hey, thanks again for Saturday evening. I was supposed to be entertaining you. It was a fabulous dinner. Are you still in the city?" She seems happy to hear from him.

"Actually no," he says. "But I will be back later this evening. Are you free for a late dinner?"

"That depends. How late are we talking here?" In a more serious voice Rebecca adds, "Is this business or just dinner? In other words, does this mean I have your account?"

"Just dinner this time, no business. Are you game?" It is obvious from not just his invitation, but the inflection in his voice that he is interested in seeing her on a personal level this time.

Rebecca takes her time in answering. There is a moment or two of silence and then. "Okay," she gives in. "I'll play your game, but just dinner and I shouldn't even accept that invitation, I don't fraternize with clients."

He chuckles, "So you've told me. Meet you at Aureole, 8:45?"

"Just dinner, Aureole, 8:45." She agrees poignantly.

"See you tonight Rebecca Webb."

"Tonight then. By the way where are you now?" There is no response and no one on the other end of the phone line. Somewhat puzzled she puts the phone on her chest and returns to her lovely view with a deep sigh.

Though puzzled, she shrugs her shoulders and finally hangs up the phone. It rings again immediately. "You're ditching me already?"

A woman's voice on the other end, "No, what are you working on?"

"Sorry Mag, I thought you were a client calling back. You never call my office line, what's up?"

"First of all, that didn't sound like your professional client voice and secondly, I've been trying your cell all morning and it goes directly to voice mail. Have you gotten my messages?"

"Maggie, I'm sorry. I have been so pre-occupied today, I don't know what's wrong with me. I must still have my phone on vibrate."

Rebecca picks her cell phone up off the desk and pushes a few buttons. "I can't believe I didn't cancel my vibrate after this mornings meeting...should be okay now. I guess I need to check my messages. Anyway, what's on your mind?"

"What's on yours? You sound strange, I don't know Bec, you sure do not sound like yourself." Maggie is a bit bewildered. It's not like her friend to be so relaxed, informal, especially during business hours.

"I don't know. I've got this new client I'm working with, well, potential client, I'm still trying to close the account and it is a big one, dream account. Anyway, he took me to a business dinner Saturday night, actually, I took him, but he ended up taking me, and he just called wanting to take me for a late dinner tonight. Am I rambling?"

"Uh, yeah. So this is another business dinner? Sounds like he likes you." Cutting straight to the chase, Maggie answers.

"I don't know Mag. You know how I am about getting involved with clients. He has been extremely professional to this point though. I think it's okay." Rebecca tries to rationalize her decision.

"Right. So, where is he taking you?" Maggie's inquiring mind wants to know. A little amused actually with the conversation.

Rebecca sighs, "Aureole."

"Well," Maggie interjects, "at least he has good taste in food and it keeps you in the hood, so if it gets creepy you can always excuse yourself to the ladies room and run home." They both laugh. "I guess stopping by my apartment after work to help me put something together for my fundraiser tonight is out of the question then?"

"No, not at all, I could stop by. I'm not meeting my client until 8:45. What time is your event?" Always eager and willing to help, Rebecca would always make time for a friend in need.

"I need to leave here no later than 6:30. I have all the prep finished, just need to run home and make the change. If you could come by, it would be really great." Most appreciative, Maggie sets the schedule.

"No problem Mag, I'll come straight from here. Should be plenty of time for us to shop your closet and have a quick glass of wine before you have to go. I'll have plenty of time afterwards to get home for a shower and change myself before my appointment."

Maggie, in her inquisitive overprotected girlfriend voice, "This doesn't sound like an appointment Rebecca, this sounds like a date. Be real. Who is this man anyway? What is the real story?"

"This is not a date, it is just dinner. I don't know much about him really. His name is Geoffrey Zandieh. He seems to be a very nice man, attractive, exceptional taste...from London. He has business interests in New York so he is here in the city quite a lot." She pauses. "There is something odd about him though. I can't quite figure him out. He is sort of...mysterious in an aloof sort of way. Not rude aloof, just... I don't know, just different."

"But attractive? Older?" Maggie is very curious.

"I don't know what you mean by *older* but no not really...probably your age," Rebecca giggles. "And, yes, I would have to say very attractive. Coiffed. Put together. You know what I mean." Rebecca describes her so-called client.

"Alright already, I won't ask any more about him. Have you heard from Patric Taylor lately?"

"No, not in a long while. I think it is finally really over. I used to get a friendly call every now and then, but not in a very long time. We are just two different people. He is very content doing his own thing. It's funny, after all these years, I don't know that we ever had anything really. How long could we have continued to play this little game of being in and out of each other's lives anyway? Though I have to admit, even after all this time apart, if he walked into my office right now, I'd still melt in my chair. What's with that anyway?"

"Melt? Please Bec. You will probably always love the guy, but I'm glad you are finally able to spend time with other men. You were meant for so much more than Patric Taylor could have ever given you. I know it makes your father happy to have him out of your life, finally and for good this time." Loving to dish on the ex-boyfriend, Maggie lends her support.

"Mmmm, your right, my father never totally approved. He liked Patric, just not for me. Anyway, speaking of Daddy, I think he may still be infatuated with you. How about coming with me out to the Hamptons this weekend. He is throwing a great party on Saturday night. I don't think he has a date, that I know of anyway."

"Please Bec. I am not quite desperate enough to date my girlfriends' fathers...yet. But I'll let you know." Maggie giggles.

"Oh, come on with me Mag. You don't have to be my father's date, I was just kidding. It will be fun. You might meet some potential donors out there." Rebecca tries to entice her friend.

"Don't count on me but I will think about it. Tell your father I said hello. Anyway, see you in a few hours?"

"Okay, see you at your apartment and don't worry about a thing. I'll have you looking like you could fund the entire organization yourself." Rebecca chuckles.

"You mean like a million dollars? How cliché." Maggie laughs. "Thanks Bec, I really appreciate your help. This is a really big night for me professionally."

"See you soon." Rebecca hangs up the phone and turns back to her beautiful view of the city.

* * * * *

CHAPTER TWO

THE CORRIDORS OF THE WHITE HOUSE can be somewhat daunting but also exciting as senior staff writer, Tim Connelly and his accomplice photographer make their way to the Press Room. Bright red carpeting, the somewhat musty smell of history and the presence of secret service pave the way. As they enter, they shake hands with their media colleagues.

"I hate this shit." Patric whispers to Tim.

"It's just part of the game my friend." Trying to make it seem worthwhile, Tim smiles half heartedly.

"I still hate it. You really dig this superficial bull shit don't you?" Patric grins knowing full well, that yes, his BFF is one of them.

Tim almost embarrassingly responds, "What...me? No, I just want to be lucky enough to get my big break and spend the rest of my life doing book signings, college lectures, guest appearances on morning news shows and raising my kid."

"I'm here for you padre'." Patric holds back laughter.

The press secretary enters the briefing room and the idle chatter of reporters greetings subsides. As the room quiets, all eyes turn to Mr. Secretary.

"Ladies and gentlemen of the press, thank you all for being here this afternoon on such short notice. The Vice President will join us shortly to make a brief statement. He asks, please, that there be no questions today after his statement as his time is strictly limited, but he and the President appreciate your being here. If you could respect this referendum, it would be most appreciated." There is a pause and a bit of low chatter in the room among the media representatives. As the Vice President approaches the podium, there is again silence. Arrogantly, he takes the stage and the microphone.

Mr. Secretary makes the introduction, "Ladies and Gentlemen, the Vice President of the United States." There is quiet and respectful applause as the Vice President acknowledges the introduction. The two gentlemen engage in a handshake and the Vice President takes the podium.

"Ladies and Gentlemen of the press, thank you once again for your patience and for being here today. I have only one brief statement and then as Mr. Secretary has already explained, there will be no time for further questions. The matter of our current involvement in Cuba, specifically Guantanamo Bay and any prisoners of the war on terror that we may be detaining there for continued questioning must be contained and therefore restricted. We, the Administration of the United States, for security reasons, find it now necessary to deem the area strictly classified and off limits to any media or any other individual without classified clearance credentials until further notice."

"Of course, with our existing embargo on Cuba, this would eliminate any media coverage of any kind in the country of Cuba until our intelligence folks inform the Administration that the restriction has been lifted and the area is once again open to media, etc. Our interrogators assure us that all aspects of the Geneva Convention will be adhered to during these interrogations, but for security reasons, and for the proper functioning of the interrogation unit, we must make the area restricted at this time. Thank you all very much and good day."

The Vice President immediately turns and exits the press room although many of the reporters and media personnel proceed in shouting, "Mr. Vice President, Mr. Vice President, just a few questions, please, Mr. Vice President." As if he has any intention of returning for questions. That point was already made perfectly clear, at more than one opportunity, but why the statement and why the early exit?

Amidst the commotion, the Press Secretary approaches the podium and thanks the crowd again for their cooperation. He too, turns abruptly and leaves the press room. Of course there is much squabbling going on between the parties left, but Tim and Patric decide to make their way out before the crowd. As they turn to leave the room, both notice a man standing at the rear of the press room along the wall with his arms folded comfortably around his waist. The man is very stoic as he is taking in the excitement in the room, but seems totally oblivious to the chatter. Obviously not a member of the press corps nor secret service, he basically stands out like a sore thumb, at least to anyone who is paying attention. Tim and Patric make their quiet exit and are directed by security out of the building.

On the way to their car Patric turns to Tim, "You know it's not like me to miss a detail, but did you notice that guy in the back of the room when we were leaving?"

"I did." Tim responds with a sense of resonance. "You're not going to believe this, but as a matter of fact, I could swear that was the guy with Becca last weekend. I wonder what he is doing here? He must be associated with her Dad or something." He pauses. "Think?"

Patric looks shocked, "That guy, with Bec? Are you frickin' shitting me?"

"She said he was a client dude. I bet he is working with her Dad on something and that's how or why he is also working with her. Makes sense, right?" Tim pauses. "You're jealous."

"He's just not her type, that's all." Patric, very quick to respond, clarifies his feeling.

"You are jealous. He's not a half bad looking guy. Maybe we should give her a call and find out what his deal is. He is definitely not media or I would have recognized him before. I wonder how he got in there?"

Making their way to the media lot, the two men get into their government issue looking rental car and Patric drives out of the secure press area .

"What do you think bud, should we hit Georgetown?" Tim says as he opens his laptop computer and starts to write. "That wasn't much of press conference, what...we were in there 15 minutes, max? It won't take long to put together my notes for tomorrow's edition that's for sure." Tim looks up at his friend. "Dude, where are you? You seem like your off in another world or something."

"Timbo, I think I've seen that guy before. I can't place him right now, but I know our paths have crossed somewhere recently." Patric can't stop thinking about the man in the back of the press room. There is something about him that is vaguely familiar and something that is not quite right.

"Next you are going to tell me you saw him in Cuba. He is a little dark, maybe he looks like a bartender at one of your favorite watering holes down there." Tim takes a deep breath and exhales loudly. "Well, I definitely saw him with your ex on Saturday night, that I am sure of."

"You're probably right, he just looks familiar to me. Why don't you get your story in, and we'll go down to Georgetown for a beer."

"Mm Hmm." Tim mumbles while typing away. "Do you get what's going on here? They just called the media off of Guantanamo. They are obviously hiding something down there."

"Here you go, always the inquisitive reporter, trying to find the grit. You never know with this Administration. Isn't that a little obvious though? The VP can't think everyone is that stupid. It's almost an invitation for someone to start looking for something. This group of jokers has never been known as one of our more illustrious administrations, but what do I know, I just take pictures."

"Somehow I feel like there is a bigger story here. The obvious is the interrogation technique debate, but that is too obvious. Maybe we should give Rebecca a call and catch up. You know her dad would probably know what the deal is. We could all get together and have a drink like the old days." Tim is getting fired up about the prospects of the three old pals getting together and if Rebecca can help with information on the story, even better.

"Tell her I said hi." Obviously Patric has no interest in the reunion gala.

"No buddy, you are coming too," Tim insists. "Come on, what are you afraid of. The three of us were great pals at one time. No reason we can't still be...pals, right?"

"No man, I'm not doing that to her and you aren't either. You call her, I know she would love to get with you and Maureen. I don't want any part of this." More insistently this time, Patric makes it clear that a buddy reunion is not a consideration for him, under any circumstances.

It had been a long time since he has seen Rebecca Webb, though he has spoken with her a time or two, but that too has been some time now. He has let go of their old love affair, which probably couldn't be summed up better than to paraphrase Bryan Adams, in a few sound bites:

"Everytime I think of you, I always catch my breath. I hear your name, in certain circles, and it always makes me smile. In your world, I have no meaning, though I tried hard to understand. But, I can't bridge this distance and I ain't missin' you at all, since you've been gone...away. I ain't missin' you, no matter what my friends say."

And he prefers to keep it that way. He can lie to himself.

CHAPTER THREE

IT IS A DARK RAINY EVENING IN NEW YORK. The shiny black water on the street is reflecting the flashing multi colored lights of the city. A cab stops at the corner of 61st and Madison where a lovely young woman jumps out in her Chanel trench coat and umbrella and runs across a few steps and down the stairs into Aureole Restaurant. Seated at the bar, there is a man who has been anxiously watching out the window for his dinner guest to arrive. His martini already perched in front of him, as he watches her every step into the restaurant. With a nod he directs the bartender to now pour that tall cool glass of Cristal for the lady he was expecting. He takes the glass towards the entrance as the hostess is helping her off with her coat.

"Let's get you dry!" Mr. Zandieh says as he hands her the glass of champagne, kisses her on the cheek and leads her back to the bar where he already has a bar stool pulled out and waiting for her to be seated next to him.

"Thanks, this is perfect," Rebecca smiles, not quite sure how to take the greeting.

"How was your day?" He asks as he admires her from head to toe.

"A little hectic" She pauses. "Sorry I'm a little late." Apologetic and a bit uncomfortable, Rebecca returns the admiration, though extremely subtly.

"And worth the wait. You are quite stunning...even soaking wet!" he toasts and they each have a sip of their drinks.

"Thank you." She laughs putting her glass down on the bar. "How was your day? You mentioned you were traveling today?"

"Yes. It has been a long day. Commercial air travel is not what is used to be and not always so convenient, but overall, it was fine." Mr. Zandieh responds to her idle conversation, with a version of his own.

"Should we be seated for dinner?" he asks, still admiring almost to the point of embarrassment to her.

"Sure, that would be great…I am starving!" Totally uncomfortable at this point, she realizes it is time to move on as she can feel his eyes looking straight through her.

Geoffrey Zandieh summons the matre'd who comes to them with two menus. They both rise from their comfy bar stools and follow him to a table for two just inside the front window on the lower level facing 61st Street. Naturally, the best table in the house. The matre'd pulls the chair out for Rebecca to be seated as she looks out the window at the wet hustle and bustle and takes a long deep sigh.

"What was that all about?" he asks.

"Sorry, it's just wonderful to sit and relax. Great table, thank you. I needed this." She pauses. "It's been a long week. Anyway, how was your day, you mentioned you were not in town when you called this morning," she comments again.

"Yes, that is true."

"You are quite mysterious tonight Mr. Zandieh. I know you said this is just dinner, but have you given any thought to my investment proposal?" Her eyes squint and she scrunches her nose as she asks.

"All business Miss Webb. This is why you need a nice relaxing evening. Let's just enjoy the evening and I promise I will get back with you on that matter later." He responds most appropriately.

"Sounds like much later." She responds somewhat disappointed.

"Rebecca, I have to be out of country and back in London for several weeks, but I will call you when I return to New York, if not before, and we will talk about finalizing your proposal then. Fair enough?" He winks at her and then begins to peruse the menu.

She gets the message and decides perhaps she has been a bit pushy for an evening that was, after all, meant to be just dinner. Realizing how inappropriate the comment was at this juncture and also realizing that it is too late to take the words back, she apologizes, "I'm sorry, you said just dinner, and I respect that. What are you going to have...for dinner?"

"Mm," he ponders. "Why don't you order for me?"

""Very cute," she says chuckling. "I'm not sure I know what you would like."

"Oh, I have a feeling you know exactly what I would like," he adds, in a most demure tone.

"Okay, Zandieh, let's keep this just dinner date on the right track, shall we?" With a smug grin on her face, Rebecca chimes back.

Geoffrey Zandieh by this time is totally enthralled in the evening and how Rebecca handles herself. As he watches her study the menu, his cell phone vibrates in his jacket pocket. Not taking his eyes off of his dinner guest, he reaches in his pocket and retrieves the phone. As he looks to see who is on the other end, his face changes from the lost enchantment of Rebecca Webb to an apologetic and serious look of "I need to take this," and he answers. "Yes, give me a moment, please." He turns again to Rebecca, "I am so sorry, but I must take this call. Excuse me for just a moment and don't drink too much champagne before I return."

He politely excuses himself and walks out into the lobby as Rebecca gives him a respectful and understanding nod. She sips on her champagne looking out the window at the rain thinking about the evening so far, and her, so-called, dinner date. What exactly is this evening about? She watches as people leave Serafina across the street, struggling to execute their umbrellas, trying to hail a cab in the rain, which isn't an easy task at this time of night.

24

Geoffrey talks for a few minutes as Rebecca enjoys the bubbly and turns her attention from the activity outside the window to her dinner companion, carefully watching him. She is intrigued, very intrigued, but at the same time, there is something that bothers her slightly. Even still, she can't help a sheepish, girly grin, "who is this Geoffrey Zandieh," she says to herself.

The waiter approaches the table, "May I bring you another glass of champagne madam? I believe that was the Cristal?"

She takes a moment to think. "Thank you. I might rather have a glass of Cabernet now to have with dinner. I believe you have a nice one by the glass?"

"Yes, several, I could bring you the wine list, but may I recommend the Duck Horn Napa Valley Reserve Cab?" The waiter has read this customer's taste quite well.

"You've read my mind, thank you, yes, that would be great. Could you bring one for the gentleman as well?"

"Certainly, madam." As the waiter departs, he and Geoffrey pass as he returns to the table and is seated.

"Welcome back. I hope everything is alright." In a most compassionate and concerned voice Rebecca is pleased of his return.

"Please forgive me for being so rude Rebecca. I had been expecting the call, but not during our evening."

"It must have been important." Rebecca is most respectful of the situation.

"Yes, it was." He pauses. "Business." Geoffrey appreciates her compassion and understanding. "More champagne?"

"Actually, I just ordered us both a glass of Cabernet. I hope that is alright," though something told her already that it was just perfect.

"I told you that you would know exactly what I like." He holds up his nearly empty martini glass and she responds in kind with her champagne. "To you, you are really quite beautiful." They toast.

Rebecca nods in appreciation and can't help but try to delve further, "So, tell me Mr. Zandieh…"

He cuts her off. "Why the formality? Geoffrey, please."

"Okay, Geoffrey, tell me, what is your business? You mentioned international brokerage, but you really didn't elaborate."

"Trust me Rebecca, you wouldn't be interested. It is really quite boring. I am just a typical international businessman who has gotten a bit lucky on a few deals. Nothing of importance. Growing up and being schooled in London, I had a lot of exposure through family connections and have been able to use that to be moderately successful. But, I am really much more interested in what you do with your spare time when you are not working." They both laugh.

"Spare time, what is that?" Still laughing, she adds, "I do a lot of things actually."

"What do you do for fun?" Not small talking, he is truly interested.

"Are you kidding, I live in New York, everything I do is fun."

"Really Rebecca, what is it that you enjoy? What makes Rebecca Webb tick?" The waiter returns with their glass of wine. Geoffrey and Rebecca thank the waiter and raise their glass to each other.

Who is this man? Rebecca is thinking. What is it about him that is so intriguing. She doesn't feel attracted to him really, or does she? He is obviously very attracted to her, or is he? She can't quite figure it out. But at the end of the day Rebecca knows that she does not want to get involved with a potential business client and does not want this little game playing exercise to get out of control.

26

"Well, I don't really know the answer to that question…many things. I do enjoy and appreciate the art of good food accompanied with a nice glass of wine and you've selected a great place for that this evening. Thank you." Complimenting his choice, she smiles.

"Cheers…and thank you for agreeing to dine with me, especially on such short notice. I really wanted to see you before I leave the country for a while." His interest becoming all too transparent.

"Will you be working in your London office?" she asks.

The waiter returns to the table, "Excuse me, have you decided on dinner?"

Rebecca returns her attention to the menu in front of her and looks at the waiter. "Yes. I would love to try the halibut and my friend will have…" looking at Geoffrey… "the same." He nods in approval with a smile. The waiter also nods and asks, "An appetizer or salad for you madam?"

"Could we share the escargot please?" Again looking at her dining companion, he is pleased. "And the organic mesclun salad for two, thank you."

"Will anyone be having soufflé this evening?" the waiter adds.

Geoffrey takes the lead at this point, "I think the lady would like a soufflé'…Grand Marinier."

Rebecca begins to giggle and smiles with approval. "Hey, I thought I was doing the ordering here!" She looks at the waiter still giggling, "that will be fine, thank you."

Geoffrey turns to the waiter, "May I also see your wine list," Geoffrey turns to Rebecca, " I think we should have a nice bottle of Bordeaux with dinner," turning back to the waiter. "Actually would you have a 1983 Chateau Haut Brion in your wine cellar?"

27

The waiter turns to Geoffrey, now quite impressed with his selection. "Yes sir we do. Bin number 469. I will bring it up right away. I am assuming you'd like for me to decant the wine for you sir?"

"Of course, thank you." Geoffrey responds. Rebecca excusing the waiter, "I think that will be all for now, thank you."

"Enjoy your evening." The waiter leaves the table and Rebecca resumes the conversation.

"Have you been to Aureole before?"

"No, but it came highly recommended. You and I both enjoy good food and I have always heard this is one of the best in the city. I have a feeling you have been here before. You seem very comfortable and at home here...good guess?"

"This is one of my favorites actually. Always good food, lovely presentation and wonderful location. Good choice Geoffrey, and not to mention... you did get us the best table in the house...not bad." The waiter returns to their table again with the decanter of wine and two fresh sparkling Bordeaux glasses which chime together as he sets them upon the table. Geoffrey tells the waiter that he will do the pouring and the waiter acknowledges with a respectful nod. Geoffrey picks up the decanter and gives it a swirl.

"Great legs," he says with a wink. Then pours the perfect amount into each glass so that the wine can breathe properly. Rebecca now swirls her glass on the table and brings it to her nose. She isn't totally sure if Geoffrey is commenting on the wine or her own extremities, but stays focused on the wine. "How is the nose Rebecca?"

"Lovely, really, a bit acidic, but that will fade shortly. You can't beat the Haut Brion. This is one of my father's favorites as well. One of my better learning experiences from him, appreciating great wine."

"Another great choice Mr. Zandieh." She remarks looking at Geoffrey, then nods to the waiter in approval. "Very good actually."

"Salute," Geoffrey holds his glass up, "to great choices then."

The waiter watches the two toast again, "Enjoy. Your first course should be out in just a few minutes." He turns and leaves them alone once again.

"Cheers, thank you Geoffrey, this is wonderful." Rebecca takes another sip of the wine and sets her glass gently back on the table to allow it to finish breathing until their first course arrives.

* * * * *

THE CAB STOPS in front of the upper east side apartment building's Fifth Avenue entrance. It is still raining fairly heavily. Rebecca pays the driver and dashes out, alone, and quickly gets under the entrance awning. She enters the building brushing the rain drops from her shoulders onto the shiny marble floors in the entry hall. The building is elegant but understated. Built in the early 1920's by C. Ledyard Blair, "The Blair House" was converted to apartments in 1928 by the famed Rosario Candela who would design and build nineteen 5th Avenue Apartment Houses. This special building offers direct unobstructed views of Central Park from each apartment. The 14 story building, now known as "2 East 70th Street" (and also 884 Fifth Avenue) has 16 apartments, mostly large duplexes and triplexes on the upper floors, but the 2nd and 3rd floors contain smaller simplex apartments that were converted servants quarters. Though modest by Fifth Avenue standards, 2 East 70th is an impressive address, and a fab find for a young single professional woman. Rebecca'a father lived in the apartment during the week while he was still practicing law full time in the city and gladly offered it to Rebecca when he retired as a practicing law partner and District Court Judge, moving on to other interests. Rebecca renovated the apartment with her own special touches and loves calling 2 East 70th home.

Rebecca runs into the marble entry foyer and greets her friend, John the doorman. "Good evening, John. Are you doing alright this evening?"

"Great Miss Webb. Wet out there tonight. How was your day?"

"Very nice, thanks. Good night John." Rebecca enters the stately paneled elevator and pushes number 3 for home. "Good night, ma'am." He smiles as the elevator doors close. He has been the doorman at 2 East 70th for over 30 years.

John the doorman has known Rebecca since she was just a little girl coming to the city with her parents. John also knew Rebecca's father very well through the years that he occupied the apartment and has a great deal of respect for him. He enjoys looking after Judge Webb's little girl and takes good care of her and her home.

The third floor bell rings and Rebecca walks down the corridor and into her beautiful apartment. It is so nice to be home ...and dry. She walks through the apartment directly to the kitchen taking off her still wet trench coat on the way and laying it over one of her chunky black bar stools. The light on the phone is blinking. She wonders who could have called the apartment. Pulling her iPhone out of her bag she notices no missed calls, while hitting the playback button on her speaker phone. A familiar mans voice is on the recorder. "Hey Becca, it's Tim. Just wanted to touch base. Hey, give us a call. Mo is really starting to look pregnant now. We'd love to see you. Maybe we could get together for a drink one of these days, like old times. Anyway, I've got something I wanted to pick your brain about if you have a minute. Give me a call when you can. Thanks Bec."

While listening to the message she leafs through some mail she left on the bar earlier, picks up her iPhone to scroll to tomorrow's calendar and types in, *Call T,* in an open spot in the morning. "Mm," she is thinking, "I wonder what's up?" She puts the phone down and slowly drags her tired body back the hallway to her bedroom.

The hallway, which she calls her Wall of Fame, is completely landscaped with family and friends' photographs, beautifully framed on the venetian walls. Photos of places and people so near and dear. Among them the beautiful island beaches of the Bahamas where her family spent winters while she was growing up. Her favorite is a large black and white of her and her mother on the pool terrace at their family home in the Hamptons on a summer afternoon. Patricia, "*Trish*" Morgan Webb was a beautiful woman, talented artist and writer who lost her battle with cancer shortly after Rebecca began her studies at NYU. She had a depth of thought, almost clairvoyant, as deep as her model like beauty. Rebecca is much like her mother in many ways, but totally unaware of how truly amazing she is.

Perhaps that is the foundation of such beauty, the innocence and naturally oblivious ambience of this lovely, articulate and unassuming young woman. Her apartment is her solace, her safe zone, her peace. The warm and cushy sofas of ivory splashed with pillows of pinks and browns. Beautiful Italian stone floors laden with plush deep brown sheep skin rugs, true comfort the moment you walk in the door. A real cook's kitchen with sparkling stainless steel, dark woods and marble veined earth toned granite. A plush ivory and turquoise peacock chair sets the stage of the big girl boudoir. The walls painted the color of the Bahamian waters, 1000 shades of blue, or so they say, though to the naked eye, it is the most complex aqua blue the mind can comprehend. Complete with girl cave laden in animal print, as every clever woman needs a fabulous closet, and feather bed with ivory duvet and peacock pillows galore. This is a bedroom truly made for a princess. The essence of her soul is in this place, perhaps that is why it brings her such peace. She is never alone as her soul is there with her and she knows it's the one place in the world that is her own. As she turns out the light and lays down in bed, another day over, she thinks about the evening, for just a moment, and within the next moment she has already drifted off to sleep.

CHAPTER FOUR

SOME WEEKS PASS as the sun is rising on a beautiful but hazy morning in late May in the city as summer is approaching and oh so quickly. On the other end of town, Patric Taylor is starting his lazy Saturday morning thinking of his trip to the islands and Cuba as he takes his steaming cup of coffee to his computer. A typical bachelor pad, the colors are dark in Patric's Tribeca loft. Dark wood floors throw off a glare of the morning light. The espresso leather sofa is disheveled, animal print pillows everywhere, trade journals, newspapers, et al, thrown at random cover the leather ottoman. A left over Heineken bottle is perched on the side table, left from the night before. He shuffles in his robe, sleepy eyed and mopey to the vintage bankers table, complete with artillery pouches, that he uses as a work desk. Loading the disk of photographs he took on the trip, he squints as his eyes take in the morning haze. It looks hot out there, he thinks waiting for the disk to load. Slowly sitting down, coffee in one hand, computer mouse in the other, Patric peruses through the photographs on his screen. What a beautiful country he thinks. At one time when Havana was in its prime and was the playground of Hollywood and Royalty, he could see what an incredible city it must have been.

The Spanish influenced and architecturally detailed buildings now dilapidated, were once vacation homes of the wealthy in a world of tropical beauty. Now they appear to be crumbling, not painted in decades nor cleaned or cared for.   Though a city seemingly still thriving on tourism from Canada, South America and Europe, it certainly does not have the aura of the Sinatra years in old Havana. A city known for music and dancing, great rum, and cigars trapped in a time warp of 50 years ago. Even the cars are from a golden era of the 1950's, though still shining, waxed and polished despite their age. To be in Havana today is like going back to that time, though the cars are the only thing that seem to be in top form.

As he clicks through the photographs, thinking of the salsa music of Cuba, Patric hits the remote for the stereo and a mix from his iPod begins to play. Still sleepy eyed, he continues to take in the beautiful shots, click by click while enjoying his coffee, sip by sip. The photos of the incredible estate that took his attention for a moment, come to the screen and he clicks through them rather quickly at first to get on to the beautiful scenery that he was actually there to photograph.

Then, wait a minute...he clicks back a few shots. Could it be? Zooming in as far as the computer will allow, the screen becomes somewhat blurry. His sleepy eyes turn into wide open eyes. This guy looks familiar, very familiar. Could it be that the gentlemen entering the car in this pic looks very much like the same dark gentleman that he and Tim saw at the White House Press Conference? Interesting that he would be in Cuba a few days or so before that press conference. "Holy shit," he yells, leaning closer to the screen "That's the dude that Tim said Bec was with? No fucking way." He sits back in his chair and laughs. "I must be delusional" he says aloud, but softly.

How ridiculous is that. No, that wasn't the initial thought at all. The initial thought was that he could be the guy at the press conference, and, that could make sense. The whole purpose of that conference was to call the media out of Cuba. Could this be the same guy? "What is this all about?" he says aloud again and reaches for his phone. While it rings he plays with the high tech optics on his computer trying to get this image as clear and focused as possible. "It can't be," he thinks, "I am just over reacting."

"Hello." a lovely female voice answers.

"Hi, Mo, how are you feeling?"

"Hi, I'm okay, I think. We will both be glad to be parents instead of parents in waiting, I am sure of that." Though excited to be an expectant mother, Maureen Connelly is ready to just be a mom.

33

"I can't even go there." Patric responds chuckling.

Also laughing, "Maybe someday. I am sure you want to speak with Tim. He is right here. Take care of yourself Patric and don't be such a stranger."

"Thanks Mo, I will be by to see you someday soon."

Tim takes the phone, "What's up bro?"

"I've been on the computer looking at some photos from my trip. You are going to think I am crazy T-man, and I might be, but I really think I did see that dude from the press conference in Cuba. Probably need better graphics, but I would almost swear to it."

"You have a picture of the guy?" Tim also in disbelief.

"Yes, I was pretty far away, but when I zoom in on the computer, it really looks like him. Are you sure this is the same guy that was with Becca?" Patric just can't get the possibility out of his mind.

"Pretty sure, couldn't swear to that, but what was this guy doing down there?" Tim just can't quite get his arms around this one.

"I shot him by accident coming out of an incredible estate, a heavily guarded incredible estate." Patric still in shock of his find.

"What kind of estate? What do you think it was?" Tim in full investigative reporter mode now.

"I don't know bro, but whatever it is, I think it is something big."

"What is a guy doing standing in the back of the room at a White House Press Conference a few days after he is in Cuba at a heavily guarded estate? Obviously, it is related somehow. He must have something to do with why the media has been shut out on this. You are right my friend, this could be something big." Tim's blood pressure begins to rise with the thought, even though coincidental.

34

"Have you called her yet?" Patric asks.

"Called who?" Tim responds somewhat bewildered.

"Becca. Have you called her?"

"Yeah, I did, a few weeks ago. I left her a message, but I haven't heard back from her now that I think of it."

"Tim, is it the same guy?" Patric not letting up on this.

"How do I know? I wasn't in Cuba and I haven't even seen your photo dude." Tim knows very well what Patric is asking.

"You asshole, is it the same guy that you saw with Bec?"

"If it is, she must have no idea who this guy is, I guarantee it."

"It wouldn't hurt you to call her back you know." Patric chimes in.

"She'll call you back before she'll call me back. Why don't you give her a ring." Tim is really digging at his friend now.

"Right, I'm going to call her about a guy that she is presumably seeing, acting like the jealous ex, just checking in on the credentials of her current affairs, which by the way are none of my frickin' business. Come on Tim, you two are as close as we ever were."

"In a different way dude. I don't know why you are so afraid to talk to her. I thought you two were on great terms."

"The best terms, man, and I want to keep it that way."

"You can't avoid her forever." Tim's unsolicited advice.

"You don't think so?" Patric fires back.

"Why would you want to? Forget I asked. I'll give her another call. At least she can tell us what the guy's name is, that would be a start."

THE CITY IS BUZZING IN THE HEAT OF THE DAY, and so is Tim Connelly. Some may wonder what this cheeky kid did to land his most beautiful and clever wife, the job he always wanted, and the beautiful office overlooking Time Square. Obviously there is more than meets the eye, or at least first impressions. Tim is a quirky young man, sweet and cute. His deep Irish eyes are wirey and wide, always observant, always aware. He's a hyper little guy, but never obnoxious with a heart of gold for his friends and family. He's excitable and charming with the enthusiasm of a young boy. And a hell of a writer which his editor saw in the first piece he wrote as an intern at the Times. Always looking for that big story.

Tim is sitting at his desk, on the edge of his seat, always ready to pop up and go on less than a moment's notice. Never settled, never laid back, he lives on his toes and it shows in his prime reporting. While doing some research, files neatly scattered in organized piles over his desk, he goes back and forth from the computer screen to the files, taking notes, preparing, for today's writing. His phone rings...

"Connelly..."

"Hey Tim, how are you?" Greetings from a most lovely voice .

"That's a familiar voice from the past, which I don't get to hear enough of, I might add. I'm doing great, how about you Bec?"

"It has been too long, Where does the time go? I'm doing well, how is Maureen? I am so sorry I haven't been by to see you guys lately. I have been so busy here." Kind and apologetic, Rebecca also misses her old friend.

"She is fine. It is a little hard to believe that we are going to be parents, scary actually, but there's something really settling and cool about it at the same time."

36

"T, you are going to be a great father. I can't imagine a more blessed child to have the two of you for parents."

"Yeah...right. Mo will be a great mom, but me? I never imagined myself as a dad, but I am excited about it."

"You'll be the best Timbo, just the best." Rebecca 's voice is calming and supportive. "Anyway, what's up. I am so sorry I missed your calls. I meant to call you back weeks ago, but I just don't' know where the time has gone."

"What are you up to this weekend?" Tim asks.

"I'm going out to my father's for the holiday. He's having his annual big deal on Friday night to celebrate the beginning of summer and it's his birthday, but don't say anything, he doesn't want anyone to know. Why don't you and Maureen come out for the weekend? There is plenty of room, it will be a great time."

"No doubt the Judge puts on a great show. I remember the parties at the house...always a good time. I'm not sure what Mo has planned, but really, let me work on it, I'll run it by the boss. Thanks for the invite. Bec, I'm working on something I wondered if you might help me with. Are you available anytime this week for a quick drink?"

"If you guys come out to the Hamptons this weekend, we could catch up there. I'm honored that you are asking for my help. Is it with a story that you are working on? I'm flattered!" Her voice is inquisitive and also uncertain. She can't imagine why Tim would need her help. Perhaps he's writing about the financial industry. It's a volatile time and an election year, maybe it is a political story.

"Actually, it is a potential story, I'm just doing my research to determine whether it is viable, but I'd rather meet with you here in the city if you have the time?" Tim's voice is serious, professional with a degree of urgency.

37

"Sounds important. I could probably meet you for a quick one today, 6:30ish? You have my curiosity up I must say."

"Well, we're kind of working on a story, not sure if it is going anywhere, but I think you may know someone who might be involved in some way." Tim lays the groundwork for Rebecca's help.

"By *we* do you mean you and Patric?" Her tone changes. It is as if you can hear her heart moving into her throat.

"Ahhh, yeah. What would you think about him joining us? Be like old times?" Tim's voice inflection demonstrates a bit of persuasiveness which is a very familiar pattern to Rebecca. She knows him well and knows when he is trying to talk her into something she would probably rather not do.

"T, this isn't another one of your, let's get Rebecca and Patric together again programs is it?" Rebecca responds with gritted teeth making it clear that she has no interest.

"Course not. It is just a story, and who better to work with on ideas than old friends. You know how much I respect your opinions and your thoughts. You have both made it all too clear that isn't going to happen, not in my lifetime anyway. I would never try to put you in an uncomfortable spot. I just think you might be able to help me on this one. So what about it? Monkey Bar, 6:30? That's on your way home and easy for me to."

"Okay, you got me. I'll be there. Tim, it's not a problem for me, really, if Patric's there, I mean, either way is fine."

"Had a feeling that's what you would say. You're the best Bec. See you later...and...I'll check with Mo about this weekend. Maybe we could make it out for just one night or something."

"Sounds great, I would love it. See you later." Rebecca ends the call.

Tim puts down the phone and smiles to himself, his familiar sheepish grin when a very tired looking Patric Taylor strolls into his office, red and sleepy eyed, but otherwise, looking like a model for Ralph Lauren. Carrying two venti cups of Starbucks, business camera case over his shoulder, he hands Tim a cup of coffee. "Who was that?"

"Your ex, Rebecca. We're meeting her tonight at Monkey at 6:30 for cocktails." Tim mentions the meeting, almost under his breath.

"Who's we?" Patric already not liking the idea.

"You and I, Padre." Tim not giving his partner a choice.

"You don't need me to ask her about her recent love interests."

"Come on man, she said he was a client. She really didn't seem all that into him to tell you the truth. I really don't think she is romantically involved with the guy." Ever assuring, Tim continues.

"You still don't need me." Patric takes a big slurp of coffee and sets his cup down on the desk as he very nonchalantly takes a seat.

"What's the matter my friend? Afraid some old fire may still flame up?" Tim can't resist the dig, he knows his friend and knows his heart.

"Right." Patric, not the least bit amused, takes another slurp.

"She said it is no problem for her. Why can't you step up to the plate my man?"

Patric leans toward the desk and takes another large sip, "You already told her I was going to be there?"

"Sure. It's really not a big deal. A cocktail among old pals. No big deal. Come on." Now encouraging, Tim knows he's got him.

"You're right. It is no big deal. I'm in for one, then I've got to head out. I've got plans tonight." Patric succumbs.

Patric reaches in his bag, pulls out a stack of photographs and tosses them across the desk to Tim. "Here, see if your researchers can find any information on these. They are a bit fuzzy since I was so far away, but there is definitely a face."

"Shit. You may be right, that could be the dude. I don't know, it is pretty blurred. How weird is this though? After we get a name from Bec tonight and any other info she might have on the guy, I'll run these down to research and see if they can come up with something."

"There is something really buggin' me about this guy."

"Jealousy, my friend, the jealousy never seems to end, does it?" Tim gets up, coffee in one hand and gives his friend a guy slap on the back with the other.

"Ease up." Patric is sensitive and knows that Tim is right. He is jealous or maybe just a bit over protective. Maybe that's part of what drove her away. Maybe the insecurity and fear of losing her was too great for him to handle. In the end, what we fear most, is usually what happens anyway, and ego or no ego, he lost her. Their love for each other didn't matter anymore, they grew apart, independently of one another and grew up, forming their own lives, absent from one another. It probably happens to most college romances, but no one ever thought it would happen to this one. Their love was a special kind, unique. Though they tried time and time again, together, and apart, it didn't seem to matter. They needed a clean break and the chance to grow completely on their own.

"Come on, let's get some work done. I've got another latte calling my name across the street." Tim grabs his jacket and the two leave the office. Tim is leading and walking very quickly in his usual somewhat high strung M.O. As they stop for the elevator Patric leans forward over Tim's shoulder, "Yeah, I can see why you need some more caffeine." They both laugh. "I could probably use another myself."

CHAPTER FIVE

DOWNTOWN IN THE FINANCIAL DISTRICT, Rebecca Morgan Webb is busy at work at her desk. Reports scattered everywhere, she glances back and forth from the computer screen to printed material taking notes in between. As her eyes begin to cross, she throws down the pen and swings her chair around to take a break moving her sight out the window towards the river. There is a knock at the door and Maggie appears with 2 white take out bags in her hands and the aroma of a Japanese steakhouse. Getting take out at a sushi restaurant is a little like getting a cup of coffee to go at Starbucks, you leave smelling like you had been in there for hours. "Sushi anyone?" Maggie continues toward Rebecca's desk with the bags. "Hope I'm not intruding. I had to be downtown this morning for a meeting, so I thought I would bring lunch."

"Great call, I am starving and really needed a break." Rebecca opens one of the bags getting out two Styrofoam cups of green tea as Maggie gets the sushi from the other bag and proceeds to make a buffet of sushi on Rebecca's desk. Rebecca tosses Maggie one set of chop sticks and the free for all begins! "How is your day?"

"I was going to call you to meet me at La Goulou for lunch to celebrate. We just finished up on the numbers from the fundraiser. Our biggest ever. Very successful. I think we broke all records. Anyway, since I was down this way, I thought I would just bring lunch to you."

"Mag, this is perfect, thank you, plus if we had gone to La Goulou, I would have never made it back to work and I really have to finish up this investment proposal by the end of the day. So, congratulations to you...on your fundraiser." She holds up her tea to propose a toast. "You looked fabulous that night Mag, just fab."

"Thanks to you, you dressed me. Anyway, it was a great success. I can breathe a little easier now with that one behind me." Maggie very craftily takes her chopsticks full of tuna sashimi directly to her mouth.

"Maggie, I have a great idea. Let's celebrate after work today. Why don't you come with me to Monkey Bar tonight at 6:30 and I'll buy you a big fat Cosmo to celebrate your success."

"Okay, Rebecca." Maggie thinks for a moment. "What's the catch, what's going on?" Maggie is suspicious of the impromptu invitation. "You are so much fun to get into trouble with, but really, what's the deal?"

"No trouble. Tim Connelly called and wants to pick my brain about something for a story he is working on, so, I told him I would meet him for a drink. Actually he and Patric are both going to be there."

"So, no wonder you need some reinforcement. When is the last time you saw Tim?"

"Actually just a few weeks ago, but only for a minute. I was at a business dinner with a client and a few other associates. Tim was there with some guys." Rebecca takes a sip of her tea to wash down the sushi.

"Did I hear he was expecting a baby?" Maggie asks.

"Yes. They are very excited." Rebecca says with a mouth full of sushi.

"Can you imagine Tim Connelly as a father?" Maggie laughs in a sarcastic but light sort of tone. Rebecca swallows and becomes very serious. "Mag, as a matter of fact I can. Tim will be an exceptional father. He will be terrific. It may put a small wrench in his social life, but T will rally just fine. I am thrilled for both of them. Maureen is a really special gal."

"She is lovely, he is a lucky guy. So, what's his story about? Success for beautiful financial planners in New York?" Maggie is curious.

Rebecca, laughing, still swallowing sushi, "Very funny. He didn't say actually. He was a little vague. Guess we'll find out tonight. Come with me. It will be fun."

"Well girlfriend, since I didn't talk you into playing hookie with me this afternoon at La Goulou, I suppose I could meet you at Monkey Bar. When are you leaving for the Hamptons?"

"I will probably leave from here at lunch time on Friday. Wish you would go up with me. Daddy would love to see you."

"Don't think I can. I may have a date Saturday evening."

"Pray tell…with whom?" Rebecca is curiously supportive.

"One of our donors. I've met him a few times before. His wife passed away a year or so ago and apparently he is ready to move on now. He hinted about maybe having dinner Saturday night."

"Hinted or asked?" Needling for more, Rebecca interrupts.

"Well, hinted, but I think I will hear from him with a formal invitation later today. He said he would call later. We'll see."

"Do we like him?" Rebecca wants to be excited for her girlfriend.

"Mmm Hmm. He is very nice, Bec. He knows your father. He said his company does their legal with your Dad's firm."

"How old is this guy?" Rebecca giving the thorough interrogation routine. Maggie has a habit of spending time with men who aren't very nice to her, at least not long term. She is a fun spirited, adorable but somewhat strong, (perhaps pushy is closer to the truth) woman, who wants to be married so badly that it frightens every good prospect and seems to attract every bad one. Especially the guys who want to fall in love for a weekend and then never be heard from again.

"I don't know…mid to late 50's maybe. Very distinguished and handsome. You will like him Rebecca. He's one of the good guys, really." She looks at Rebecca with a girly grin and they start cleaning up the Rebecca's desk.

"I just want you to be happy Mag, that's all."

"I know my dear friend. Listen, I am going to get out of your hair so you can finish up your work. I'll see you at 6:30." The girls have a friendly girly hug and kiss on the cheek. Maggie leaves the office as Rebecca's phone rings.

"Rebecca Webb. (pause) Yes, in fact, I was on the line to Zurich early this morning. Everything is fine and should be set up and ready for you before the end of the business day today. How is Mrs. Stobart feeling?" (another pause) "Your very welcome, thank you John."

She hangs up the phone and starts to get back into studying the reports on her desk. Just another day of business in the city and she loves it. The phone rings again, and this time, the interruption is not as welcomed. With a deep sigh, she throws the pen down on the desk and thinks aloud "will I ever get this finished?" then answers. "Yes, Rebecca Webb."

"Good afternoon Miss Webb the very lovely Miss Webb I might add." The voice, a familiar somewhat sexy british accent.

"What a surprise, I thought you were out of the country?"

"I am. I still have a few weeks of business to finish up, but couldn't help checking in with my financial planner. How are you doing? What are you up to these days?" Mr. Zandieh expresses his interest.

"I am actually heading out to the Hamptons this weekend to spend some time with my father."

"The Hamptons...sounds nice. What does your father do there?"

"Enjoys life mostly now. He is semi-retired."

"Semi-retired? That sounds rather nice." Geoffrey Zandieh is looking forward to slowing down a bit himself.

"Yes," Rebecca responds. "He was an attorney in the city for many years, but he hasn't practiced in some time now. In fact, the attorney who referred you to me actually works with my father's firm."

"I should have guessed that you are the daughter of an attorney."

"What is that supposed to mean? I guess you are going to give me a great British barrister joke now?"

"No..." laughing, "you are quick on your feet, that is all that I was implying."

"Very funny." Rebecca is not laughing and not very amused.

Sensing her lack of interest in where the conversation is going, Geoffrey Zandieh gets back on track. "Rebecca, I may be able to swing through New York on my way back to London. Would you have dinner with me? I would love to discuss further your proposal."

"I would also love to discuss my proposal further. Are we getting close to finalizing it? I would like to be able to get things working for you." She sounds impatient and she knows it. Is this guy really going to do business with her, or is he just looking for another excuse for a dinner date?

"I apologize Rebecca. As soon as I finish up on this project, I promise, we will finalize our business dealings. I really have not had much time to thoroughly review it, but I will get to it soon. How about I give you a ring when I am on my way to New York and we can finalize it then. Deal?" He senses her impatience and tries to appease her.

"You have yourself a dinner date, Mr. Zandieh. Safe travels."

"Talk soon." Zandieh disconnects the call.

She hears the click and realizes the connection is gone. Oddly as it seems, the call does bring a smile to her face. Now back to work.

* * * * *

FROM THE BACK SEAT OF A DARK SEDAN, Geoffrey Zandieh dials his cell phone. "It has been handled." There is a pause. "Yes. I am on my way there now. I don't think it will be a problem. Everything is under control." There is another pause. "Yes. He is getting a bit restless, but fortunately, he doesn't really have a better option at this time." Pause. "Thank you, I'll be in touch."

The sedan pulls into the drive of the familiar Cuban estate. The lush landscape drapes over the entrance way as the rays of sunlight gleam through the car window. The car stops under the portico at the entrance and is greeted by the familiar welcome committee. They open the door for Mr. Zandieh and he is directed, once again, to the back veranda where the man awaits with one fine Cuban cigar in his mouth. He offers Zandieh another. "Mm. Cohiba Millennium Reserve, not bad, thank you." Zandieh obliges.

The man offers a light, which Zandieh takes to light his cigar and the two men are seated. It is another gorgeous day in the tropics outside of Havana, though a bit warm, the fans and trade winds keep the veranda quite cool. Puffy white clouds float across a beautiful deep blue sky. "Enjoying your summer?" Zandieh asks of the man.

"I am not complaining about the view, you understand, but how long are they going to want me to stay here. I thought this deal would be complete by now."

"You are to stay here until the time is right. It will work out sooner rather than later. You will get your freedom and the Republicans will get their election. Right now, try to be patient and enjoy the view just a little while longer." Zandieh must keep his guest comfortable and patient for just a little while longer. The end is drawing near and he can taste it. He is as anxious to get this deal done as his impatient guest.

46

"You know I could leave here at any time, if I wanted to. They still do not appreciate the scope of my power." The man obviously means what he is saying and is saying exactly what he means. Zandieh is only the courier, the middle man. He has a fiduciary responsibility to both parties of this deal but cares about neither one.

"There is no need to make threats. They could have killed you 10 times over already and yet after all of these years, here you are, living in this most beautiful place, like a king, about to have full amnesty. Be patient, this will work out for everyone. It is all part of the game. Remember your family. It is worth your life and worth their peace. Play their game. Meanwhile, try not to get a sunburn." Zandieh is chuckling, trying to make light of the situation, a situation that is only dark and about to become even darker.

The man puts his cigar down into a pewter tray on the shiny marble cocktail table. "I need a computer to do some writing."

Zandieh puts his cigar down in the tray next to the mans, "Are you crazy? You know that is not possible."

"What am I supposed to do with my time?"

"Meditate. Pray. Read." Zandieh gets up and walks toward the door. He nods at the guards and is approached by another guard who appears to be in charge. "He is getting restless. Get him something to read. Perhaps a novel or two. He probably hasn't read a meaningless bit of fiction in a long time. Keep him content, whatever it takes. He is asking for a computer, this is not possible. He made a deal, he will fulfill his end of it...period."

"When will you be back?" asks the guard.

"When they send me for him...should be soon. Keep him busy and keep him here. We are all being paid quite well to see this through."

"Yes sir, we are doing our best." The guard tries to reassure.

SIRENS ARE SOUNDING, HORNS BEEPING, just another busy afternoon on the streets of New York City. Walking quickly to get off of Fifth Avenue, Rebecca turns down 54th Street toward the red awning marking the entrance to the Monkey Bar. Once a favorite mid town hang out of she and her friends, it's been a while now. It is still a bit warm for early summer in the city, but she is cool in a fitted white stretch linen V-neck shift, white linen Manolos and Damier Azure handbag. The bar is somewhat crowded with after work cocktailers, but Tim has a great table just inside the door on the window to 54th Street. He is waiting alone with a Heineken as Rebecca looks around for a familiar face. Tim stands and waves his hand from around the door. "Hey gorgeous, what's up?"

Rebecca quickly gets to the table and the two embrace. Tim gives Rebecca a fond kiss on the cheek and they both sit down. "Hey to you!" She puts her bag on the back of the chair and takes a deep exhale. "It's been too long since we were out for drinks, just us guys!" chuckling. Tim also belts a laugh and nods.

"Hope you don't mind if Patric shows up. He's working on this story with me, but knowing him, he probably won't show anyway."

"I don't mind a bit, I told you that. It would be great seeing him and also for the three of us to share a cocktail again. Like old times...college days...they seem so long ago Timbo! Where does the time go now?" Rebecca reminisces.

"You are not kidding. Isn't that Maggie Pearlman?" He says looking toward the door.

"Oh...hope you don't mind. I asked her to join. We have also been trying to get together for a drink, so I mentioned to her to come by, hope that's okay."

"Sure..." Tim says in a questioning tone, "I thought you'd just want to be with the guys!" He laughs again.

"You know Maggie, she will be at the bar working the room anyway." Maggie approaches the table and shakes Tim's hand, "Hi Tim, nice to see you. Congratulations on your soon to be fatherhood." She turns to Rebecca and leans over to give her a girly kiss on the cheek as she sits down at the table.

"Thanks Maggie. Nice seeing you. I read the piece on your big fundraiser in our paper the other night. Sounds like quite a success."

"It was, thanks Tim. Oh, excuse me for a minute you two, there is Paul Weinstein. Would you guys mind if I had a moment with him. I've been trying to track him down for weeks."

"Of course not, we have some business to discuss."

"Thanks Bec, would you order me a cosmo...back in a few." Maggie's attention is totally on Mr. Weinstein at this point, and both Tim and Rebecca are both relieved to have a few minutes alone to talk before Maggie gets back. The cocktail waitress finally makes it to the table for a drink order. "Can I get you something ma'am?"

"Sure," Rebecca pauses, "I'll have a Kettle One Cosmo, could you bring two, one for my girlfriend also."

"Anything else for you sir?" The waitress turns to Tim.

"No thanks. I am good for now."

"Okay, I'll be right back with the Cosmos." She turns and leaves the table.

"What's up T? What's with this story and how can I help?" Rebecca is genuine in her interest and a little bit excited to be able to help a friend. She has always loved Tim, like a brother, and always admired his intelligence and veracity. It feels good to be in an old familiar place with an old familiar friend.

And, the feeling is mutual. Tim has adored Rebecca from the moment they met in college. They have that special friendship that is rare between a man and woman; never insecure, never a sexual thought, always respectful. A brother-sister kind of love, innocent adoration between male and female friend, so special and so rare.

"Bec, I don't know where to start, except to just start. I need to know about the guy that I saw you with some time ago at Balthazar. You mentioned that night that he was a client. Interestingly enough, he seems to have popped up right in the middle of a story that Patric and I are working on together. We were assigned to a press conference in DC, and your new client was there, not as a member of the press or media, in fact, not seemingly a member of anything, but he stood in the rear of the press room and seems to be a part of this story in some fashion. Anyway, I was hoping that you could shed some light on exactly who this guy is."

"Washington?" Rebecca is confused and bewildered at this question. Washington DC, what would Geoffrey Zandieh be doing at a press conference? He's never mentioned being associated with the media, or the government, especially the US government. She feels a pit in her stomach and the temperature of her face beginning to rise.

"Do you know who I am talking about Bec? Do you know what your client does for a living or what kind of connection he may have to Washington?" Tim persists in his questioning.

"His name is Geoffrey Zandieh and I guess I don't really know that much about him. He is actually a little vague about that part of his life, but his financial credentials are very sound. He is from London and was referred to me by an attorney in my father's firm, though he didn't know that his attorney worked for my father, or did at one time anyway when he was still actively practicing. He has been speaking with me about investing and setting up an off shore trust. He has only mentioned that he is a, quote, *international broker of sorts*, and would be spending some time here in New York."

"He said he wanted to work with someone here who was familiar and in touch with international markets which is how he was referred to me. He did mention briefly that he did some work with the government, but as I said, he is very vague. I think I may have his business card." She fumbles through her handbag and finds her card folio. Leafing through it she finds Zandieh's card and hands it over to Tim. "I wasn't sure I had it in here. As I mentioned, his current address is London, but I do know that he has met with a realtor and is looking for something here in New York as well. I think he is doing a good deal of traveling right now."

"When is the last time you had contact with him?" Tim continues.

"He calls on occasion, to check in it seems. I am trying to finalize our dealings, but he has been distracted with a project he is working on. I really don't know much more than that. I met with him at my office only a couple of times, then the business dinner at Balthazar when you saw me with him which was really a coincidence. He actually showed up there alone that evening and when I saw him, I invited him to join my group. I thought it might help close him on my proposal. That's when I saw you. Then...I did have dinner with him one other time, I don't know, a few weeks or so after that."

"Mmm, business dinner?" Tim examining Zandieh's business card as if he is going to find some clue, coding, something on the card. "Geoffrey Zandieh, Shoreham Group, Ltd." Tim reads the card aloud. "Bec, are you dating this guy?" He looks her straight in the eye.

Interrupted by the waitress who returns with the drinks Rebecca looks up at her. "Thank you." Then she turns back to focus on Tim. "No, nothing like that. It has been strictly platonic and professional. I do suppose though, if I were to be totally honest, I might say somewhat intriguing."

"Bec, I am so sorry, that is really none of my business, sorry, really."

Tim apologizes and as he looks up notices Patric, fashionably late, coming through the door and decidedly ends this direction of the conversation. As Patric floats toward the table, Rebecca turns around and watches him approach. Almost in slow motion he arrives, kisses her on the cheek and takes a seat. "Hello beautiful." He has such a classic elegance for a man, casual, comfortable and confident. A rather stunning JFK, Jr. look. As he is seated, she melts in her seat. Trying to hide it she looks back at Tim.

"Better late than never Padre." Tim feels Rebecca's heart sinking, he knows both of them, far too well.

"Sorry man, I got held up." He looks at Rebecca. "Sorry."

"How've you been? Tim tells me you two are working together again. Very cool." Forcing conversation, Rebecca looks up at him.

"Doing great, just great. How about you?" Patric responds.

"Fine, really. Tim and I have been talking briefly about the story. He said it might have something to do with a new prospective client of mine." She gets right into it, not missing a beat, and not about to let him know that her guard has been totally disengaged. What is it about this man that she can't let go of totally. Yes, he is brutally handsome, charming, talented, endearing, kind, loving, all of the above, but for her, it is much more, much deeper and something that a) she can't explain, and b) would rather not feel. She really thought she was beyond this point, until now, until he walks into the room and lights up her spirit. It is as if there is no one else now in this crowded bar, except the two of them. Well, of course Tim, he has been part of the two of them since the beginning.

"I guess Tim mentioned that we saw him in DC at a press conference dealing with the Gitmo issue, well I guess Cuba in general, and Tim mentioned that he thought you may know him, that's all." Tim hands Patric the business card to review.

Patric takes the card, looks at it, but doesn't really even read it. "This is kind of eerie, the three of us sitting here, like the old days, except you wouldn't have been caught dead drinking one of those pink drinks back then Bec." Laughing at her most civilized pink drink.

She laughs, "You're right. I can't drink many Heinekens anymore."

The waitress returns to the table to wait on the newcomer. "Sir, would you like something?"

"Heineken, bottle, thanks." He looks at Rebecca and winks. "Some things change and others just don't I guess." He is smiling, looking directly at Rebecca. Though his tone is somewhat in smart ass mode, he still can't take his eyes off of her either.

"Okay you two, we are all still friends, right?" Tim chimes in feeling the tension between them.

"Absolutely. Tim, I'm sorry I wasn't very much help for your story."

"Hey, Bec, you were great help. At least we have a name. Would it be alright if I held on to this business card?"

"Sure." Rebecca takes another sip of her cocktail.

"Are you planning to see this guy again Bec?" Tim asks while Rebecca just about chokes on her cosmo. Clearing her throat, "Probably. I did prepare an investment proposal for him and I do plan to close the deal." She says with conviction.

"Well, if you get into a conversation with him about what he does to earn so much money for you to invest for him in off shore trusts or whatever, let me know, would ya?"

"Sure T..." she rolls her eyes and can't help laughing. The business woman in her arises, as the investigative journalist in Tim also comes to the forefront. "Would you two excuse me for a minute?"

She grabs her bag and heads toward to stairs leading to the ladies room. Patric's adoring eyes follow her every step of the way. As Tim is talking, Patric never takes his eyes off of her.

"She sure looks good man." Tim takes a swig of Heineken.

"Yeah...she does that, always has." Patric also takes a big sip and pounds the bottle down on the table.

"It is so obvious that you both still have it for each other. Why can't you two just get it together, man?"

"Too late my friend. She wouldn't be interested in this cat anymore, her tastes have changed, obviously." Patric smiles sheepishly as he looks into her empty cosmo glass. "Is she dating the guy or what?"

"She said not. But she did say he is mysterious and intriguing, whatever that means. She might be able to get us some inside partner."

"Yeah, he is making a play for her." Patric assumes.

"You're jealous." Tim calls Patric out on his presumptuousness.

"Bull shit." Patric takes another slug of beer and again slams the bottle on the table.

"You are so jealous." Tim knows his friend well and can't help but rub it in as deep as he can. Tim would love nothing more than to see his two best friends in life patch up their differences and move on to the mature family life that he has chosen now. He reflects for a minute on how cool it would be for he and Maureen, Rebecca and Patric to be raising families together.   Maggie returns to the table to find the two gentlemen chatting it up.

"Hi guys...what happened to Rebecca? Did you scare her away already." She looks directly at Patric.

"Very funny. Nice to see you too Maggie." He gets up from the table.

"I'm outta here. T, I'll catch you at your office manana. Hi Maggie, later Maggie." Patric gets up to leave.

"Don't leave on my account. This was just getting good." Maggie snears.

"Stay and finish your beer at least. How do you think Bec would feel if you left before saying goodbye. That would be totally rude." Tim calms Patric down a bit.

"That would be rather rude." Maggie says in her best bitchy, smart ass tone.

"You are both right. Sorry, just have places to be. So, Maggie, what' s up with you these days?"

"Still raising money for the needy." She says proudly.

"Maggie is Director of the Arthur Reese Foundation." Tim adds.

"Oh, right, I do remember reading somewhere that the Reese Foundation had a record breaking event sometime recently. A friend of mine donated some artistic photography for your auction. I think they were black and whites of Central Park." Patric is back in the conversation and charming as ever.

"Oh yes. Ashley Sabian...they were fabulous photographs. How do you know Ashley?" Maggie is very interested in this answer.

"She is just a friend...professional acquaintance. We collaborated on a couple of projects in the past couple of years."

Rebecca walks back to the table and sits down as girlfriend Maggie gives her *the look.* You know the look from one girlfriend to another saying, *don't even go there sister,* as she feels the magnetism across the table. "Is anyone having another?" Rebecca asks.

"I'll have one more." Maggie turns and looks for the waitress.

"I need to get going. Bec, it was really nice to see you. Please give your father my best." Patric gets up and walks to Rebecca. She also gets up and they have a warm embrace. He kisses her again on the cheek and turns toward Tim. "Thanks for the beer, pal. I've got a commitment tonight or I would have another with you fine folks." Patric chuckles. "Later guys...Tim, I'll see you in the morning sometime...bye Rebecca." Their eyes lock again, only for a moment, and then she quickly looks away.

"Take care Patric. Say hello to Ashley for me. Tell her I will be calling her again for a donation." Maggie wants to make a point to her dear friend that there is another woman in Patric's life, even though she has no idea to what extent. She just wants to wipe that silly girlish grin off of Rebecca's face and protect her from any more heart ache as it relates to Patric Taylor. Patric never turns back or acknowledges Maggie's comment.   He raises his hand waving goodbye behind his back and leaves the bar. Of course, Rebecca watches him float out, just as she watched him float in. She knows she needs a distraction, and this little game she is playing with Geoffrey Zandieh might just be the ticket to moving on, completely.

"I should probably head home myself. Bec, thanks again for coming. It was great the three of us having a drink and everything. Listen, if you get with that client of yours again and he mentions anything about what he is working on, would you give me a call?"

"Of course T. Do you think he may be involved in the Guantanamo Bay situation in some way?" Rebecca is also quite curious.

"I have no idea, but I'm going to find out what is going on down there somehow." Tim says with journalistic conviction.

"Tim, always the investigative reporter." Rebecca laughs.

"Like you said earlier, some things never change." Tim gets up and goes to give Rebecca a hug goodbye.

"Touche'...tell Maureen I said hi. Give her a big hug for me. I hope to see you two out at the Hamptons sometime this summer."

"We will sure try. Thanks for always inviting us Bec. I hope it works out, if not for your dad's birthday, maybe over the fourth. Next summer we will have a little one to bring out to the beach. After the baby comes maybe things will get back to normal for us."

"Tim, after the baby comes, things will never be normal... as you know it anyway." Maggie puts in her two cents.

"Yeah." Tim is chuckling. "It will be different.   Nice to see you Maggie. Good luck with the foundation."

"Thanks Tim, best wishes to you and Maureen as well."

Tim grabs his navy sport coat off the back of his chair, throws some cash on the table for the check, "That should cover it." He gives Maggie a friendly hug and Rebecca an affectionate little brother kiss. She responds in kind. Tim, throwing his jacket over his shoulder, gives the girls a friendly wink and leaves the bar.

Maggie turns to Rebecca. "So, what was that all about?"

"Strange actually. They saw Geoffrey Zandieh, my new client, at a press conference in Washington. I can't figure out what in the world he might have been doing there." Rebecca motions for the waitress.

"Why don't you ask him next time he calls?"

"Yes, I will ask him. He might actually be coming to New York soon. He mentioned he may be in town and would like to get together, hopefully to finalize his account."

The girls order another drink and ask the waitress to bring the tab. It is getting very loud and lively at Monkey Bar now as the girls enjoy their fresh cosmos.   The pianist starts to play an old familiar jazz standard. Rebecca looks at Maggie, "God, I love New York!"

The Monkey Bar, established in 1936, at the Hotel Elysee on 54th Street for decades has been a hang out of young and old, media barons and after hours politicians. It is decorated by an Ed Sorel jazz era mural which amidst the painted "monkeys" are some 60 caricatures of those who made the era great. Writers like Hemingway and Scott Fitzgerald with Zelda, of course. Tennesse Williams who met his untimely death there. Magazine publishers Alexander Woolcott of Vanity Fair and Henry Luce of Time, Life, Fortune, Sports Illustrated, and Conde' Nast. Mayor Laguardia and of course the Chairman of the Board, Frank Sinatra. Ella and the Duke, Cole Porter, George Gershwin, Louis Armstrong and Billie Holiday. Even Rebecca's favorite, Richard Rodgers, whom in collaboration with Lorenz Hart wrote her favorite song, *My Funny Valentine*, among many others with Oscar Hammerstein. Rodgers is still one of only two artists ever to be honored with a coveted Oscar, Grammy, Tony and Pullitzer Prize. Rebecca loved this era. A time when gentlemen never left the house without a tie, and a pair of white gloves was stock merchandise in every woman's handbag. Maggie leans over toward her friend, "Are you okay?"

"Of course, I'm fantastic, what do you mean?"

"Seeing Patric. Were you okay with it? I could feel the tension and could see the way you two still look at each other. I just wanted to make sure you were alright." Maggie puts her hand on Rebecca's arm gently as if to comfort her in time of need.

"Oh stop. I've never been better. It was great seeing him actually. I am okay with it, with all of it. We have our own lives now. It's all good. Thanks for your concern, but unnecessary." She holds up her glass to toast to her friend. "Love ya Mags, thanks for the concern."

"What are friends for? You are always there for me Rebecca. I just don't want to see you hurt anymore, especially over him. I am glad you have moved on."

CHAPTER SIX

REBECCA IS DAYDREAMING AS SHE DRIVES her white 500 SL convertible into the driveway of her father's beautiful South Hampton estate. The grass is deep Kelly green and landscaped perfectly, not one blade of grass is out of place like a plush New Zealand wool carpet. The white fences aligning the driveway are adorned with flowers of every color of the rainbow and highlighting the entrance to Drew Webb's country manor estate. Two golden retrievers come running from the front door down the driveway to greet the car.

"Hi guys...where's Daddy?" Rebecca takes her bag from the back seat and walks toward the front door with the dogs where she is greeted by the housekeeper. "Hi Yvette. Is Daddy home?"

"Hello Rebecca. Yes. The Judge is in his study waiting for you. He has been so excited that you are coming up this weekend. Can I get anything for you?" The two walk into the house together as Yvette takes Rebecca's bag.

"I'm fine right now, thanks Yvette. I'm going to go check in." She walks down the hallway through the double mahogany doors and enters the study. The sun light from the large arched windows is almost blinding at this time of day. She can see a silhouette of a man at the desk through the glare looking out the windows. The interior of the room is dark with mahogany walls and a fabulous view through the arched French doors out to the pool terrace and tennis court. She walks around the desk, puts her arm around her father and plants a big kiss on his cheek. "Hey handsome, what are you up to?"

The Judge gets up and greets his daughter with a big daddy bear hug. "Glad to see my girl. How was your week? Any new big deals?"

"I'm working on a pretty big one right now. An off shore trust for a fairly large portfolio. It is good business if it pans out."

"Sounds interesting. Where did you find this one?" Drew sits back down in his office chair and Rebecca sits on the corner of his desk.

"Interestingly enough, from your firm. One of the young trust attorneys referred him. He is a bit mysterious really, but has been a pleasure to work with."

"What do you mean mysterious?" a protective father asks.

"I don't know. He is very bright, interesting, has the funds, he's just a trifle vague about where they come from. What is even more baffling is that Tim and Patric wanted to meet me for a drink last week to ask about him. They said they saw him in DC at a press conference regarding the Guantanamo issue. Very strange. He did mention doing some work with our government, but very casually and I didn't get the impression that it was recently."

"Where is this gentleman from Rebecca?"

"London. He said he is an international broker of sorts. I just assumed probably large acquisitions. I would say that he is probably of Persian heritage, but London born and raised. Highly educated both here in the states and abroad. He is somewhat intriguing. His name is Geoffrey Zandieh, ever heard of him?"

"Mm. Not that I recall. I'll have him checked out. You aren't thinking of mixing your business with private life are you my dear?"

"Daddy! Of course not. Why would you say that?"

"Just the way you said he was intriguing."

"I meant in an intellectual way." She responds very poignantly.

"Well, I think we should find out a little more about him before you spend too much more time being intellectually intrigued. Walk out to the pool with me." Drew opens the French doors to the terrace.

Father and daughter walk arm in arm through the lush gardens to the pool patio. An ice bucket with champagne awaits on one of the white wrought iron tables next to the pool house. The sun is now beginning to set and the warm orange glow on the pool reflects on the windows of the pool house.

"I love this time of day. The colors are so vibrant. The house looks fabulous this summer Daddy...just beautiful."

Drew pops open the champagne and pours them each a glass. "Here you go my dear."

"Thank you. Happy Birthday weekend! It is so good to be up here. I have needed a break." She takes a sip. "Mmm, delicious. What's on the agenda this weekend?"

"Well, I thought you and I would go out for dinner in the village tonight. I have some business associates coming for lunch tomorrow around one and then Yvette will prepare for just a small dinner party here tomorrow night."

"A business luncheon on your birthday? I suppose you haven't told anyone that it is your birthday have you. What are you working on anyway? Can't business wait until next week?"

"Just some political volunteer work, no big deal. It won't take long and then we'll have the afternoon to get ready for our dinner guests tomorrow evening. It will be great fun. I haven't entertained as yet this summer. Thanks for coming up for the old man's birthday."

"Who is coming tomorrow night...anyone special I need to know about?" Smiling, Rebecca pries her father for the scoop.

"Do I have a date, you mean?" He blushes.

"Well...???" She gives her father the raised eyebrow, inquiring minds want to know look.

"As a matter of fact, I do have a lady friend joining us. Let's sit down." They both take their glass of champagne to a lounge chair. "She's pretty and nice and bright. You will like her Rebecca. She was a publisher in the city and retired out here after she and her husband divorced last year."

"She sounds lovely Daddy, can't wait to meet her. I am so glad that you have someone special to spend time with."

"No one could ever replace your mother. She is my true love."

"I just want you to be happy. You have so much to offer someone and I don't want you to spend the rest of your life without someone to share it with." Totally offering her full support.

"Don't worry about me angel, what about you? Any new man trying to steal my daughter from me that I should know about?"

"No, not at the moment. It was nice to see Patric last week. He looks good." Rebecca stares off into the distance rather nonchalantly.

"Looks were never his weakness," comments the protective father.

She rolls her eyes, "He is working with Tim on a story for the Times. I think he is still doing some freelance artistic work as well. He is very talented, Daddy."

"That's what you have always told me sweetheart. I am sure you are right. Patric is a nice young man, I just never thought he was quite good enough for you, that's all. You can't blame a father for wanting the best for his little girl, can you?"

"Of course not, Daddy, and I love you for that, among other things. I'm going to go hop in the shower and get ready for OUR date night." Rebecca gets up and kisses her father on the forehead.

"Okay, Princess. I'll see you for dinner." He watches as his lovely daughter strolls back up the hill toward the house.

THE SOUTHHAMPTON ESTATE OF THE HONORABLE DREW WEBB was his and wife Patricia's dream home which was previously owned by Tricia's parents. Designed by Grosvenor Atterbury, this turn of the century country estate was inspired by the great Lasdon Estate at Cobbling Rock Farm in Westchester County. Complete with white clapboard siding, hunter green shutters and of course an American Flag always hanging from second floor terrace over the entryway. Not as grand in scale as its inspiration, Morgan Manor boasts 17 rooms including exercise gym, theatre, 4 bedrooms and 6 bathrooms. Not to mention sweeping staircases and lovely entertaining areas. The sun-filled rooms all have southwest exposed French doors which open onto a large terrace leading through the gracious lawn and gardens to the pool, tennis court and gazebo.

The gardens are lush and provide lovely privacy around the borders of the property. A short block walk to the beach and very close to South Hampton village, it was the home the Webb's dreamed of spending the rest of their lives in together entertaining friends and family, hosting their daughter's wedding one day, and spending summers playing with their grandchildren. They were only to enjoy the home just under five years when Tricia became ill, and within a short year and a half, she was gone. Drew Webb was not unfamiliar with this kind of pain after he and Trish also lost a young son to cancer but he was absolutely devastated by his wife's illness and death, and after her passing, dedicated all of his time and efforts into his posts with the CIA and the Homeland Security Council. His work and service for the country became of utmost importance and kept him busy enough to overcome his loss and sorrow. After a few years, he retired from his post as Director and returned to the Hamptons where he continues to practice law on a selective consultation basis through the Manhattan Law Firm where he began his career just after graduating from Harvard Law School and remains a partner. Drew Webb is a fine and honorable man, attorney and judge. Above all, an exceptionally true loving husband and a wonderful and supportive father.

Rebecca loves coming home to the Hamptons. After a nice morning with her father, Rebecca decides to hit the gym. While she is getting her hour of cardio on the EFX, she remembers the summers here growing up as an awkward teenage beauty. As does every room in the house, the exercise equipment also views the beautiful back lawn down to the gazebo and pool house. As she huffs and puffs with Rick Braun and Richard Elliott's, *R&R*, playing loudly in the gym, she sees her father's luncheon guests begin to arrive and make their way to the gazebo. Yvette already had a beautiful lunch prepared and everything set up for their meeting.

Four very distinguished looking men, well dressed but casual and very serious looking join Webb and shake each others hands taking their seats for lunch. Rebecca watches through the window and tries to recognize any of the gentlemen, but the only one familiar is the executive editor of the New York Times, Bill Weller, who has been a family friend and very close friend of her father for years. The two men met in Washington and became fast friends in the early 1980's when Weller joined the New York Times at the Washington Bureau while Webb was appointed and serving as director of the FBI.

Drew Webb's career began in Manhattan as a young city attorney fresh from Harvard Law, and quickly worked his way to a post as a New York City Judge and eventually to the US District Court for the Southern District of New York. There he specialized in a life long passion, prosecuting New York mafia families and because of the national recognition of his vast success he was appointed director of the FBI in Washington and then ascended to the CIA. During this time he continued to hang his license to practice law with the firm of Rooney, Stein, Rosen and Chaffee in Manhattan where he eventually became one of their senior managing partners and continues to sit on their board of directors and serve in a consulting capacity. He loves the law, every aspect of it. From small town legislature to international terrorist law, he thrives on justice and honor.

Rebecca, breathing heavily and sweating profusely, finishes her workout and walks down the hall, sweat towel around her neck, and up the stairs to her bedroom to shower and change. She thinks aloud, "I wonder what he is getting involved in now?" and she begins to giggle. Dressed for the afternoon in a casual Prana print dress, she comes through the house and pops into the kitchen picking out an apple from a bowl of fruit on the kitchen counter, "Buongiorno Yvette. Come sta'?"

"Buongiorno Principesci. You look so pretty today Bella."

"Thank you. I am going to drive into the village for a while and do a little shopping and visiting. Could you let Daddy know where I am if his meeting finishes up before I get back?"

"Piacere, of course I will. Have a nice day."

"Do you need anything from town?" Rebecca takes a big bite out of her apple.

"No. Grazie mille. I have everything already for tonight. Thank you Rebecca, Ciao."

"Great. I will see you later this afternoon. Ring me on my cell if you think of anything. I won't be too long. Arrivederci." Rebecca loves speaking Italian with Yvette. She is from a little village northeast of Venice in the Friuli region, close to Udine. She came to New York as a child with her family who legally immigrated to America and has worked for the Webb's since Rebecca was a little girl. Yvette taught her to speak Italian as a little girl, but after being away from home so many years and not practicing, it does not come as easily as it once did. Rebecca walks out through the front door, gets into her SL in the drive as Yvette watches her drive out of sight. Yvette, who never had children, adores Rebecca as if she were her own.

* * * * *

IT'S A GREAT SATURDAY AT SHEA STADIUM, hot, humid, the smell of burned popcorn, over cooked hot dogs and beer in the air. The Mets are hosting the Cardinals for a great Memorial Weekend four game home stand rivalry and Tim Connelly scored 2 Times box seats for this, the second game of the series. As much as he would have wanted Maureen to have the second seat, he felt it is probably much too hot for a young pregnant woman to endure. That was his recommendation anyway, that it would probably be better for her if Patric took the other seat for today's game. Not as big a Mets fan as his friend Tim, Patric is kind enough to accept Tim's invitation, plus a day at the ball park Memorial Weekend is a great New Yorker tradition. The guys arrive early for the first pitch at 2:10 to have a beer while taking in batting practice. Tim can't wait to watch Albert Pujols crank a few out of the park and he is hoping, as a life long Mets fan that he does it plenty in practice and not during the game.

"Nothing beats a cold beer on a hot afternoon at Shea. Thanks man, this is great." Patric holds up his beer cup to his friend.

"Pleasure dude, maybe the beer will help. You look like you are big time hung over...late night?"

"I didn't sleep. I haven't slept. Can't stop thinking about what that guy, what's his name, Zanderly, what he was doing in DC, Cuba. Did you find anything out yet on this dude?"

"It's Zandieh, British chap and no. We can't find anything on him. Nothing under that name anyway. It just doesn't exist at least on the first layer, research is going to dig a little deeper for me"

"Tim, what is going on, and how in the hell did she get in the middle of it?" Patric sounds both perturbed and concerned.

"I don't think she is in the middle of anything. You heard her, she doesn't even really know the guy. She said she is going to close her business deal with him, maybe she can get more information."

"Do you think he knows who her father is?" Patric looks at Tim.

"If he is involved with our government in some way, there is no way he couldn't know exactly who he is. It is interesting that he was referred to her by a trust attorney in Webb's firm." Tim responds very methodically, almost as if to be putting pieces of a puzzle together. He realizes it may have been no coincidence that Zandieh found Rebecca to do his financial planning.

"We need to go back to Cuba. I know where they are hiding something, or someone and we are going to find out what it is." It is obvious that Patric is now totally committed to this project.

"Spoken like a true investigative reporter, you are starting to sound like me my friend. I must be rubbing off on you after all of these years. You never gave a shit about any of this crap before." Tim is excited about his friend's interest, but knows the interest lies much deeper than a story for Tim's column. "I think I see what's really happening here."

"Right, cut the bullshit T, there is something to this, I know it. I know that's the same guy. Don't you find it interesting that the White House is calling the press off Guantanamo, or Cuba in general for that matter, basically forbidding anyone from any kind of investigative reporting, and this guy, who is at the press conference, came in from Cuba very recently and very conveniently. We are going down there to find out what is happening at that place. You in?"

"We need to talk to my editor." Tim is trying to have a sense of reason and pragmatism, rules guy that he is.

"What do we need Weller for, you don't have a story yet?"

"You don't sound so sure about that." Tim fires back.

"Okay, I'll go back down there for a few days and see what I can come up with, then we'll go to your editor." Patric is determined.

67

"You can't tell me that your motivation here has nothing to do with Rebecca Webb." Tim grabs Patric's arm and turns his attention away from batting practice.

"Come on, I told you that is all over." Patric insists.

"Patty my boy, I saw the way you look at her...still. It is far from over with her, why can't you just man up and admit it."

"Get off my shit, okay? I'm just trying to help you out, and I don't have a lot of other work knocking down my door right now so I have a little time. Plus, I need to get to Nassau and check on my boat. Hurricane season is coming and I need to make sure she is tied down properly. I can head down in the next week or two. You don't need me for a little while, right?"

"Be careful man. I don't like the way this thing is starting to smell. I can find another great photographer for a few days, but not another best friend. You need to watch your back side, right. If this is as big as we think it might be, there must be huge surveillance. It was a fluke you got so close the last time, I don't see it happening twice. You were lucky once, you're not going to be so lucky again."

"I know what I am doing man. I'll be careful. I met some people there who will remember me. I will try to get us some real solid information and then we can have something to take to Bill Weller." Patric is serious and Tim knows it.

He is even a bit impressed with his old pal's tenacity and he knows that if there is going to be a story breaking, the only place to find the answers is in Cuba. "Okay. Remember though, Weller isn't just my editor, he is also a very close personal friend of Drew Webb. He will definitely want to get Webb involved especially when we tell him that Rebecca is associated with this dude, professionally or otherwise."

"Yeah, right, whatever. Right now, we have a story to catch for you padre. I will look into flights tonight when I get home from the game. Sure you won't consider coming with me?" Patric looks at Tim for a response, Tim shakes his head. "The things I do for you buddy." Patric winks at Tim and taps his near empty beer cup against Tim's. "Now let's get another brewsky and a dog before the game starts."

* * * * *

It is a beautiful summer evening at Morgan Manor. Drew has Frank Sinatra piping throughout the house and Yvette has candles and fresh cut flowers from the garden everywhere. Everything looks lovely and the aroma of garlic coming from the kitchen smells fantastic. In addition to being a wonderful housekeeper, Yvette is also a fabulous rustic Italian cook, surely preparing a favorite fresh pasta. Rebecca comes down the winding stairs in a beautiful floor length Missoni halter dress. The zig zag stripes of ivory, black and gold are a perfect compliment against her beautifully golden tan skin. She sashays down the hall to the study, where she knows she will find the birthday boy.

"My darling, you look stunning, just like your mom." He admires.

"Thanks Daddy. Where is your date?"

"She should be here anytime now."

Rebecca hands her father a beautifully wrapped elongated pear shaped package with a lovely ivory silk bow tied around it's neck. "Happy Birthday Daddy!"

"What's this?" he says opening the package. Obviously a bottle, he looks at Rebecca bewildered, jokingly, as if he doesn't know what's in the package. "Romanee Conti 1989. Rebecca this is quite a vintage."

"And so are you..." she gives him a big birthday hug.

"I'm not sure if that is a compliment or not," he laughs. "Thank you."

"Only a small token of love to my favorite guy in the entire world and of course, it is a compliment. You are truly the finest man I have ever known. Thanks for everything you've done for me. By the way, what was your meeting about today at the gazebo? It looked very intense. Does it have anything to do with the election this fall?"

"Oh, just some governmental issues that I am trying to help with. We need some change in this country Rebecca. This is a very important time in our history and a very important election. We are in quite a mess as a country and I am just working with some very bright people to see if we can help get things back on track. It keeps my mind stimulated, you know. Nothing you need to be concerned about." The doorbell rings. "That will be Leslie, let's go give her a proper welcome shall we?"

Drew and Rebecca walk arm and arm to the entrance hall. Yvette is busy in the kitchen, so Drew opens the door. A very beautiful 50ish woman is standing in the doorway in a lovely white summer gabardine shift. Drew embraces her with a kiss on the cheek.

"Hello Rebecca. So lovely to finally be meeting you."

"Darling, this is Leslie March." Drew seems proud to introduce his lady friend to his daughter. Rebecca can sense that the two of them are very fond of one another and she is thrilled.

"I've heard so much about you and though I've seen a lot of your photographs around your father's home, you are much more beautiful in person." Drew leads Leslie into the house as the girls shake hands.

"It's so nice to meet you. I am glad you could be here to celebrate the occasion. Daddy, why don't you two go out to the terrace and pour some champagne. I will check on the kitchen and put the note out for the rest of the dinner guests to come on out to the terrace for drinks. I'll be out in just a minute." Rebecca leaves them alone.

"Drew, she is just lovely." Leslie knows how much his daughter means to him.

"Did you expect anything less? She reminds me so much of her mother. I hope it is appropriate for me to say so." Drew is almost apologetic in his comment, not wanting to hurt Leslie's feelings in any way.

"Of course it is...and of course I expected her to be wonderful." Leslie puts her arm inside of Drews and rests her hand on his forearm as they stroll through the house out onto the terrace.

The night is clear and mild, the stars are beginning to shimmer brightly throughout the sky. The full moon is bright, and illuminates the back lawn and gardens like a bright spotlight from the heavens. The lighted pool reflects it's waters motion on the side of the pool house and gazebo as if to mimic dancers on the patio.

Drew pours Leslie a glass of champagne and then himself. "You look absolutely lovely this evening, Leslie. Thanks for coming and for being so gracious to Rebecca. It means the world to me." He takes a taste of the champagne. "It has been so long, I really don't know what is proper in this situation You will have to forgive me from time to time I am afraid."

"Happy Birthday, Drew. I am very happy to be here." Leslie and Drew sip on their champagne and enjoy the view through the garden to the pool house. "It is a beautiful evening for a celebration." Leslie looks at Drew and he takes her hand to his mouth and kisses it ever so gently on the back of her soft palm.

* * * * *

CHAPTER SEVEN

A FEW WEEKS PASS AND SUMMER IN THE CITY is heating up. Though there was a reprieve from the heat for a week or so, now the summer haze lies like a blanket over Manhattan. The air is thick and the humidity is high. The same holds true of the markets. Rebecca, plods along continuing to make deals and watch the unstable and volatile summer markets. She knows the game Wall Street is playing this time of year and is just trying to keep her clients interests safe until things stabilize after Labor Day. In addition to the normal weekly rise and fall of the summer market, a continual sliding trend has appeared and there is talk of imminent recession. The days are stressful, but Rebecca's dogmatic approach to the protection of her client base and their interests also lends a challenging environment for which Rebecca Webb thrives. She is all too familiar with this summer game and with the 4th of July fast approaching, it will get even worse and less predictable until after the Labor Day weekend marks the change in season and Wall Street returns from the Hamptons back to the city to work.

Hopefully, the naysayers are wrong about what's on the horizon though the sub prime mortgage markets are flailing with no relief in site which seems to be affecting the entire market. It is Thursday, just after noon and Rebecca takes a deep sigh as she watches the end of week sell off begin. She picks up her cell phone to make a call and it rings in her hand. She doesn't recognize the number, but answers anyway. "This is Rebecca."

"Well hello Rebecca. How are you?"

"Fine, I'm fine. Sorry you took me off guard for a moment. I didn't recognize the number, but I don't think you've ever called my cell. Are you back in New York?"

"Actually I'm back in London. I've been traveling quite a lot and needed some time at my office to wrap up a few things here."

Geoffrey Zandieh has somewhat of an apologetic tone to his voice. "I am sorry I haven't been in touch, but, I have reviewed your proposal in detail and I am finally ready to move forward and get some funds in your hands."

"I am delighted to hear that Mr. Zandieh. I thought perhaps you had found yourself another financial planner. The markets are a bit fragile this summer, but it is a good time to lay our ground work and take advantage of some very competitive buy ins." The professional Ms. Webb is in full business mode.

"Actually Miss Webb, I was thinking of something a little more casual. What are your plans next weekend? Are you free? Could I possibly dominate your business card and dance card for a few days?"

"A few days?" Rebecca is bewildered and very much taken aback. This is not at all what she expected to hear and she is not in any way prepared. Of course, she has been propositioned by clients in the past, but at this moment she can't recall ever having one quite so forward as this one. Maybe it's the European influence, most Europeans that she knows tend to have little in the scruples department and just call it like they see it. There is something that she appreciates, about this bold and raw honesty, but in this case, for the first time in her professional career, she is uncomfortable.

"I know it's a lot to ask Rebecca, but I do very much enjoy your company and I do want to finalize our deal, so I was thinking, I have to make a stopover in Nassau for a bank meeting and wondered if you might like to spend the weekend at the Ocean Club. Separate rooms, of course." He continues with his proposition.

"I thought you were being rather presumptuous." She is not amused at the moment, but she does love the Bahamas, especially the Ocean Club. How bad could a few days in paradise be?

"It's a beautiful spot, I think you would really enjoy it," he adds.

Mr. Zandieh still trying his persuasive best.

"Yes, I am familiar. I do love that beautiful blue water." She is picturing the beautiful white sand beach, Tiffany blue clear water, palm trees swaying in the tropical breeze. Okay Rebecca, she is thinking, get a hold of yourself here. It is ridiculous that you would even consider the possibility of going to the Ocean Club with Geoffrey Zandieh.

"Then you've been there?" He seems surprised.

"To the Bahamas? Yes. My family had a home there for a number of years, though we haven't been there as a family for some time. Since my mother passed away."

"Oh, I am sorry to hear that Rebecca. I was hoping that I might perhaps be tempting you with a few days in a never before seen paradise. Once again, I underestimate the lovely Rebecca Webb. Perhaps you are not ready to go back to the Bahamas." He sounds disappointed, even deflated.

"Actually, it might be a nice break. Though it has been some time, it was very special to our family. Could you give me some time to think about it, before you call the next potential travel companion on your list. When is your meeting?"

"What do you mean next one on the list?" He laughs.

"I am quite sure your little black book has few empty pages."

"First of all young lady, I don't have a black book as you call it and I haven't had a relationship with a woman in a long time. My business has taken most of my time in recent months, even years really. I have, however, very much enjoyed spending time with you. Though it has been somewhat limited and strictly professional, you like sparring with me. You are a challenge to me, you are different and I like that"

"When are we talking about ?" She is unimpressed with his rhetoric.

Geoffrey knows this is not going exactly as well as he had planned and also can sense that she is not impressed. "I can be quite flexible in the scheduling of my meeting. What is your schedule?"

"I will be going back to the Hamptons over 4th of July holiday, but I could probably sneak away for a weekend later in the month."

"Alright then. I will email you airline arrangements...say leaving Laguardia on a Friday afternoon after your 4th of July holiday and returning on a Monday morning?"

"I haven't accepted your kind invitation as yet Mr. Zandieh, Mr. Very Confident Zandieh." There is a pause, silence on both ends of the phone line, then she laughs, breaking the ice and letting him know that she has been playing with him just a little. "A Sunday evening return would be better for me?"

"That didn't take very long." He seems pleased.

"What?"

"For you to accept my, how did you say it...kind invitation."

"I didn't say yes as yet, but if I do, returning on Sunday night would be better for me." She keeps the suspense going.

"Sunday night. Fine. Take as much time as you need to get back to me, but not too much time. I've got to move on to other matters for now. I'll be in touch soon and look forward to seeing you in paradise!" Feeling somewhat confident she will join him, he ends the call.

"Byeeeee." Rebecca gives a long salutation and puts her phone down. There is a knock at the door as her assistant peeks in opening the door very slowly hoping not to be interrupting her boss.

"I have the documents you asked for regarding the wire transfer to Deutch Bank in Zurich." She approaches Rebecca's desk.

"Thank you. Listen, we can finish up later this afternoon. Go have a nice lunch and thanks again for all of your help today." Rebecca excuses her assistant who has been working very hard for her this morning and through the lunch hour.

Rebecca's assistant makes her way to the office door and turns around. "I hope you don't mind me saying, but you have a glow I haven't seen on your face in a while."

"Really? I don't know why?" Questioning herself. "Funny, though, this Geoffrey Zandieh that I have been working with is mysteriously flirting with me. I'm not exactly sure what his agenda is. At times he is so professional and strictly business, and then others...I don't know. He does intrigue me, but he doesn't be still my heart if that makes any sense. Silly I know."

"Maybe it's just his game that gives you the glow. You always like a challenge." Rebecca's assistant is very familiar with her competitive spirit.

"Maybe. Yes. He is that, if nothing else." She laughs. " I've been trying to get his business finalized for months. Anyway, I'll see you after lunch."

The assistant leaves and closes the door quietly. Rebecca looks out the window towards the river, to which she often relies on for good advice. It would be nice to get away from the city for a few days, she thinks. His game, what is it? Too strange...she looks at her watch, "Oh shit, I am going to be late meeting Maggie for lunch." She quickly gets up and throws her handbag over her shoulder. Running out of the office, she puts her sunglasses on and calls the building concierge to arrange for a taxi to meet her at the front door, hoping the traffic heading up town is not too bad today. She promised Maggie she would not be late.

* * * * *

An impatient Maggie Pearlman is waiting at a table on the street at La Goulou on Madison Ave. with two glasses of Rose' wine. It has been the favorite lunch spot of the two girls since they have known each other and, sadly, they have heard that the building is to be razed. Maggie looks at her watch and picks up her cell to make a call. At that moment, a rushing Rebecca Webb exits a cab not 6 feet away from where Maggie is seated. Maggie puts her phone down, "I was beginning to think you blew me off today."

"Sorry Mag, I got tied up at the office and lost track of the time. Forgive me? I sent you a text on my way here."

"I got it, and of course I forgive you. How was your weekend in the Hamptons?" Maggie is happy to see her cohort in crime.

"Gosh Mag, I can't believe I haven't talked to you since then. Where does the time go? It was a great celebration weekend, rather low key for my father, but wonderful. He has a new friend!"

"Do tell...do we like her?" Maggie always loves a good scoop.

"You know Mag, I really do. She is beautiful and seems very nice. I think Daddy is actually a bit smitten, though he is trying to hide it and brush it off as casual friendship. I am so happy for him. It has been so long since my mother passed away. I can't believe he really hasn't had real female companionship since. So, how was your hot date?" Rebecca also anxious to catch up on Maggie's weekend dis.

"Dates...and fabulous. We had a wonderful time at dinner, and he has already taken me to lunch since." Maggie is all smiles, ear to ear, almost blushing. It is obvious to Rebecca that she really likes this man. "What are you up to the next couple of weeks?" Maggie asks.

"I'm pretty busy in the office right now. With this uncertainty in the market and the normal summer unpredictability, everyone is pretty stressed. The banks are all struggling. Very volatile situation."

Rebecca continues. "These triple A rated bonds that are tied to the sub prime mortgages are beginning to look like junk bonds. This is really going to have an affect on most of my clients and the Street in general. Actually, it is going to affect the entire world. I don't know what to put my investors in now, really for the first time since I've been in the industry." She pauses. "Sorry to get off on that little tangant, I guess I am more pre-occupied with it than I thought." She takes a sip of wine. "Delish, thanks Mag...anyway, I'll be going back up to the Hampton's for the fourth and then Geoffrey Zandieh has invited me to join him in the Bahamas for the weekend later in the month. What's up with you?"

"Who? " Maggie nearly chokes on her Rose'.

"Geoffrey Zandieh. Client. I know, it's breaking all the rules."

"You have dinner with the guy once, business dinner, and he is already asking you on a weekend rendezvous in the Bahamas? Only you have that affect on a man. What have you done to the poor guy?"

"He said there would be separate rooms, business, no pressure." Maggie looks at Rebecca with a smirky grin, as if to say, come on, you are smarter than this princess. Rebecca shrugs her shoulders back at Maggie. "What...he said we would have separate rooms."

"How do you feel about that?" Maggie is trying to help her friend think through the obvious. She might be a cracker jack financial planner for the wealthy, but maybe not so smart in matters of the heart, or the dating game anyway.

"You know, as curious as I am about him, I really don't have any desire to be intimate with him. It's strange. I do enjoy talking and sparring with him, but I can't imagine going any further than that. I can't explain it. There is just something about him." She sighs.

"You don't sound very sure of yourself Miss Rebecca."

.

"Mag, I don't know if I'm interested in him or if I just don't trust him at all. Does that make sense? Anyway, he said we would stay at the Ocean Club and I do have friends there that I could visit if he gets to be too much, right? I haven't seen a lot of my friends there since mother died, it would be nice to catch up with them."

"You don't need an invitation from an interesting Englishman to do that. You could go to Nassau anytime you wanted." Maggie pauses to have a sip of wine. "So, are you going to go meet him?"

"You are right about all of the above, and I have no idea what I am going to do." Rebecca stares at her wine glass as they are approached at the table by a tall, young and very hot French waiter.

"Can I interest mademoiselles in lunch?"

"Yes, please. Bec, are we having the usual?" Maggie looks at her friend for approval.

Rebecca nods, "Absolutely."

Looking at the gorgeous French waiter Maggie orders, "We'll have one Caesar salad to share, one order of mussels and one order of truffle fries," the waiter is busy writing,"...and two more glasses of Rose', s'il vous plait. Merci." The waiter nods and walks off.

"Maggie, I know why this is our favorite lunch spot." They both watch the young Frenchman walk away. "And the food is very good too!" They laugh and toast their glasses. "Good choice Mag, I love a good crisp Rose' in the summer. I will miss this place."

"Me too, and, you have to admit, they are all so cute and cut!"

"You are a mess Maggie. I meant the restaurant! So what's up? What did you want to talk to me about?"

"The common area of my apartment building is being renovated."

"They will be doing my floor later this month. It's going to be such a mess." Maggie laments.

"Do you want to stay with me until they are finished?"

"Would you mind? I would only stay until the demolition phase is done. It shouldn't be more than a week or two at the most." Maggie is excited by the offer, even though she knew Rebecca would comply.

"Of course I don't mind. It would be great to have the company. We will be great roomies. It will be fun." Rebecca sounds as excited as an 8 year old about to have her first sleepover.

"That would be great Bec. I owe you. Lunch is on me today."

"That is not necessary, but, I will happily accept this time." Rebecca smiles and has another sip of Rose'. "Thank you."

"So...back to Nassau, doesn't Patric keep a boat down there?" Maggie is right back on it, having accomplished her goal for the day already.

"I think so, I'm not really sure, he used to." Rebecca seems very cool and wondering why Maggie would bring this up. "Patric has nothing to do with whether or not I decide to go to Nassau."

"I know, so why wouldn't you go. You have an interesting man, with funds, not that it matters, but doesn't hurt, a weekend at the Ocean Club, friends to escape to if need be, I say go for it."

"Actually if I decide to go, it sounds like it would correspond with your renovations so you would have my apartment all to yourself for a few days. And you are right, I should go. I don't know why I am so suspicious of him. He really is a charming guy." The girls are interrupted by their tall, dark waiter with lunch and two more glasses of Rose'.

"Lunch doesn't get any better than this! Thank you." Maggie gives the waiter her approval and the girls enjoy their fabulous lunch.

CHAPTER EIGHT

PATRIC TAYLOR IS BACK IN THE BAHAMAS on his 42' Beneteau in Hurricane Hole Marina. It has been a couple of months since his last visit to the beautiful island and his pride and joy, the Mer Soleil. He tries to spend time on the boat at least four times a year and he keeps her in perfect, pristine condition. The islands of the Bahamas are beautiful for sailing, especially in the summer when the waters are calm and the trade winds constant. After rearranging his duffle bag, careful to pack his camera safely between layers of clothing, Patric goes up on deck to enjoy the sunset and a cold freshly opened Kalik, the king of beer in Bahamas. The water is calm and glows of the pink sun, palm trees sway ever so slightly in the mild breeze preparing for the end of another day. His cell phone rings. "Hey Tim, what's up?"

"Just checking on you bud...you set for tomorrow?"

"I'm on a 7 am Habana Air flight. I've already made arrangements for a helicopter tour of the island. One of the bartenders that I met last trip has a brother in law that is a heli-tour operator and he hooked me up. I plan to make it quick and get as many shots as I can from the air. I'm going to try to get back here tomorrow night on the last Habana Air flight. Hopefully I will be able to get enough in one day."

"Be careful amigo. If we are on to something...and I think we are, it could get hairy. Are you doing this for the story, or for Becca?"

"What are you talking about?" Patric disregards the thought.

"Forget it, I'm sorry. Just be safe. Call when you can."

"You got it. Don't worry, T...piece of cake. Later." Patric puts the phone back in the pocket of his cargo pants and returns to his Kalik and this incredible sunset over Nassau Harbor. He can't help but remember the many evenings spent on Mer Soleil with Rebecca. It was a pretty special time, but now, only a time gone by.

He thinks of one night in particular, some years ago when the sunset was even more perfect than this one and very romantic. Shaking his head abruptly back into reality, he enjoys the setting sun.

* * * * *

ON THE OTHER SIDE OF THE ATLANTIC, Geoffrey Zandieh walks into an office building in downtown London on a gloomy, rainy, typical London summer day. He is wearing a very stylish Burberry Raincoat, a necessary stock item in London, brushing the water drops off of his shoulders. As he enters the building, he greets a very attractive and buxom young receptionist. "Good Morning, Chestine. You are looking lovely as always." He sets his umbrella down, props it against her desk and takes off the raincoat draping it over one arm.

"What brings you into the office on this dreary day?" She asks.

"Just catching up on a few things. Do you have anything for me?"

The lovely Chestine looks at Mr. Zandieh with her sexy Brit bedroom eyes, "Nothing here. I did confirm your arrangements as requested at the Ocean Club as well as the first class air itinerary for Miss Webb. I am assuming it is MISS WEBB?" She pauses. "Is she pretty?"

"Stunning actually, and yes, it is MISS WEBB. Would you e-mail her itinerary to this e-mail address with a note that I will meet her at the library at the Ocean Club for afternoon tea at 4:00 on that Friday afternoon." Geoffrey hands Chestine Rebecca Webb's business card.

"I will take care of it, Mr. Zandieh. It is nice to see you again. You don't come by this way much anymore. You've been busy then?"

"Yes. I am just finishing up a big project actually, and then I plan to take some much needed time off." He takes a deep breath.

"With Miss Webb?" Chestine asks while her eyes are focused on the business card. "I'm sorry that is none of my business, now is it?"

"Very funny. It is a business trip Chestine, otherwise there would have been reservations for only one room." He walks past the reception area to the elevator, and enters the open door.

When the elevator door opens, he exits down a long mahogany paneled hallway to a large mahogany door. There is no name or number on the door. He unlocks it and enters a very nice large office filled with beautiful English antiques, a Louise XIV desk and beautifully crafted bookshelves filled with books on both interior walls. Geoffrey deposits the umbrella in a large brass umbrella stand and lays his coat over one of two very large leather wing back chairs that sit on top of a fabulous antique Persian rug of every color imaginable. He walks past the desk to the window and opens the draperies exposing a fabulous view of London town in the rain. His cell phone rings.

"Yes. I am on top of the situation. I don't think you will need to worry about that. By the time he is able to get the information together, we will have our insurance policy in place." Pause. "I understand." Geoffrey lays the phone down on his desk, sits down and leans backward in his chair, with his hands interlocked behind his head. With an accomplished grin on his face he takes a deep breath and a long stretch, exhaling ever so slowly.

He knows this job is soon to be complete and he can not wait. This is the last deal that *international broker* Geoffrey Zandieh will be involved in. He described a long deserved vacation, what he meant was retirement. And the thought has crossed his mind, that perhaps, Miss Rebecca Webb could be part of his life when all of this is behind him. He thinks of her and hopes that one day she will understand and will also want to have him in her life. It is a beautiful and perfect thought, in a perfect world anyway.

* * * * *

THE HABANA AIR DASH 8 LANDS SMOOTHLY at Havana International Airport, Havana Cuba. Patric Taylor exits the plane with the other 38 passengers from Nassau, mostly Bahamian men going to the city for rum, Cohiba cigars and young women. There are two other men traveling together who Patric assumes are partners and also American, and a young Bahamian family going to Havana on vacation. Though embargoed by the United States, Cuba still does plenty of tourism business from other countries. Many Canadians and Europeans find escape from cold winters in Cuba and South Americans seem to love the beach resorts, Cuban food and elaborate shows. Patric clears customs and asks the agent not to stamp his passport. The airport is mass chaos with tourists looking for currency exchange, ground transportation, tourism information, etc. Patric is approached on the other side of customs by a young Cuban gentleman. "Are you Taylor?"

"Yes. Patric ...please. Are you Carlos?"

"Si. My brother-in-law sent me for you. You want to see our beautiful island from the sky?" Carlos reaches for Patric's duffle bag to carry though Patric holds up his hand as if to say, I've got it.

"Si. I'd like to take some aerial photographs. Is that possible?"

"Si Senor. No problem. Habana is most beautiful from the air."

"Muy bien. Can we go now?"

"Si. Follow me senor." The two men walk through the airport where a 1950's red Ford pick up truck is waiting out front. They drive to the other side of the runway to the private jet and heliport.

"I hope your bird is in better shape than your truck." Patric says laughing to break the ice and start a conversation.

Carlos also laughing, "Si Senor. You don't like my truck?"

"I take very good care of her. She is over 50 years old." They park and get out of the truck. Patric throws his duffle bag over his shoulder and they walk out onto the tarmac to what is clearly Carlos' helicopter. Climbing aboard, Carlos hands Patric a headset and after securing it, Patric begins assembling his camera in his lap. Carlos starts the engine, checks the instruments, makes a few notes in his JEPS manual and obtains clearance for takeoff.

As they begin their ascent Carlos asks, "Did you have a specific area in mind?"

The voice is a bit muffled through the headset especially with the noise of the propeller. "Yes Carlos. I want to go just east of Habana to the beach area. Nice homes there. Are you familiar with the area?"

"Yes. Very nice homes along that beach. Mansions for Cuba."

"Yes. It is beautiful. I have shot the Botanical Gardens in the area when I was here on my last trip. That is when I met Phillipe. I wanted to try to capture the beauty of the area from the air this time."

"Not a problem, senor. I don't know how close I can get you to the gardens...but I will do my best. We are carefully monitored, so I will have to stay within the flight pattern guidelines."

"Gracias Carlos." As they fly around and past the Botanical Gardens and beach area, Patric begins shooting. He points to the area close to the estate that he remembers. Carlos shakes his head no.

"This is as close as I can get. That area is restricted."

"Why?"

"I don't ask questions Mr. Taylor, I just stay within my flight plan."

"Of course Carlos, I understand." Patric is disappointed and puts a super zoom lens on his camera and starts taking shots of the estate.

"Carlos, what is that place over there?" Patric points to the estate.

"No se'. I don't know. Casa grande si?"

"Muy grande! Are you sure we can't get a little closer? I would love a shot of that. My friends wouldn't believe someone could have a house like that one!"

"I will try to get you a little closer, but only for un momento. These people do not like air traffic over their homes and many are with the government." They get closer to the estate and as usual there is a gentleman sitting alone on the veranda with what is obviously posted "caretakers" at all doors to the estate. There is a privacy wall built around the property. Patric is clicking as fast as he can, just hoping to get something good within the momento of time that he will have. Carlos gets a call on the radio, and they turn sharply as he is strongly asked to leave the restricted area immediately. Patric shrugs his shoulders as if to say, "whatever," and Carlos pulls the helicopter back around the beach.

"What was that about?"

"I told you Senor, these people don't like air traffic and we are not going to question it."

"Okay. I think I have some great shots of the gardens and coastline. Let's put her down and stop by Phillipe's place. I'll buy you a beer."

"Si." Carlos is laughing and appreciates the offer which he will, of course, take. While Carlos is concentrating on the landing Patric takes the memory card out of his camera and replaces it with another. He puts this one inside his pants folded in the band of his Tommy Hilfigers and removes the lens from the camera packing each piece neatly back into his duffle bag. The two men exit the helicopter and walk towards the FBO. As they enter, they are stopped at the door by a Cuban Officer.

"Que 'esta' en la bolsa?" (What's in the bag?)

"Is there a problem officer?" Patric plays the stupid tourist. He is hoping the officer does not assume he is American. Fat chance right?

"La bolsa por favor." (The bag please)

"He wants your camera bag, Senor." Carlos tells Patric, though Patric knew exactly what the officer was asking for.

"Si." Patric says looking at the officer and hands the bag over. The officer puts the bag down on a table in the FBO lounge area and opens it, removing all of the contents. When he takes out the Tommy Hilfiger underwear Carlos and Patric look at each other with raised eyebrows and quietly laugh.

"Sir you are welcome to inspect everything in my bag, but…" Carlos stops him giving him a "*Shhh*" sign placing his index finger over his lips.

The officer carefully examines each camera piece and lens. He takes both the battery and memory card out of the camera. "Usted es libre de dejar." (You are free to leave.)

Patric starts to say something and Carlos grabs his arm, again asking him to keep his mouth shut. The officer walks away with the battery and memory card in his hand. "Gracias Oficial." Carlos thanks the officer for letting them go, turns to Patric and they quickly walk out of the FBO to Carlos' truck.

"I am sorry about your camera equipment Senor Taylor, but I was afraid we got too close to the restricted area."

"I am sorry to waste your time Carlos or to put you in a bad spot here. Will you be okay?"

"No problem. We were lucky all the official wanted was your camera equipment. Is bueno. You still pay me, without pictures, si?"

"Of course I pay you Carlos. I should pay you double for your trouble. Let's go get that beer!" They now are laughing, despite the fact that both men were sweating bullets back at the FBO. Carlos drives to Old Town Havana, Old Habana, to an outside café/bar on the street where Phillipe is working. He is happy to see them arrive and puts two cold beers on the bar.

"Hola Senor. Did my brother-in-law cuide buena de tu?"

"Si, gracias Phillipe. Good to see you again. Thanks for hooking me up with Carlos."

"Dos Equis?" Phillipe pushes the two beers across the bar to Carlos and Patric. He reaches below the bar, where he is hiding his own beer.

"Phillipe, gringo camera de la jardin al este de la playa y cuando llego la policia llevo a su equipo de camera."

"Por que'? Que' sucedio?" Phillipe asks his brother in law.

Patric interrupts, "I don't understand. But they took my pictures and the battery to my camera. There won't be any more pictures this time. Phillipe there is a house out there on east beach, este de la playa, casa grande."

Carlos interrupts, "Mansion."

"Yeah, mansion. It has a wall around it and looks like it is guarded or something. Do you know anything about it?"

"No Senor. No se'." (I don't know)

"I wonder if it has something to do with why they took my camera equipment?" Patric takes another swig of his beer.

"I ask around amigo. If I hear something, I let you know. How long you stay in Habana this time?"

"I go back to Nassau tonight. If you do hear anything…"

"I try Senor." Phillipe interrupting Patric. "You never know."

Patric turns to Carlos. "Gracias Carlos. Thanks for today, great flying. You are a very good pilot. Cuanto?"

"Two hundred US."

"US cash is okay?" Patric is surprised.

"Any cash okay, Senor." Carlos takes the money. "Gracias, y para la cerveza, dos equis. I am sorry you did not get your pictures."

"That's okay amigo. Thanks anyway. Carlos, could I get a ride back to la aeroporto?"

"Si senor, tengo el placer." The men finish their beers and shake hands.

"Adios Phillipe. You have my cell number if you do hear anything." Phillipe nods. "Thanks again for your help. Bien mi amigo. Hasta luego." Patric shakes Phillipe's hand and throws a very nice tip on the bar as Carlos starts the truck. The smell of leaded gas fills the air as the truck backfires on the street. Patric laughs as he gets in the truck.

Thrilled to have gotten away with the memory card in his underwear, so far anyway, Patric is anxious to get to the airport and comfortably seated on the flight back to Nassau. It has been a stressful afternoon, though he has played it cool, inside he was scared to death. Thinking to himself, "God, please get me back to Nassau safely," he tries to relax for the ride back to the airport. It wasn't a totally wasted trip, that is if there is anything good on the memory card. Right now all Patric can think about is getting out of Cuba and back on the Mer Soleil. Then he will be able to exhale. The adventure of the day has been exhausting and as Carlos hits a bump in the road, Patric, a bit startled, realizes he has dozed off. "Come on now partner, stay alert," he says to himself. "This is no time for napping."

CHAPTER NINE

IT IS ANOTHER STELLAR SUMMER WEEKEND in New York and the Hamptons are gearing for what is sure to be a fabulous 4th of July holiday celebration. No one more than The Honorable Drew Webb who spends most of the summer planning for his infamous 4th of July party. Needless to say, patriot that he is, 4th of July is his favorite day of the year, and no expense is spared for his holiday gala in the back lawn at Morgan Manor. White lights are strung through every tree, the pool is lit with beautiful floral and candle floats, hundreds of white candles everywhere. The orchestra is set up in the gazebo and the guests will dance the night away around the pool terrace. This black tie event is second to no other in South Hampton and the highlight of the summer for Drew Webb.

It is mid afternoon, Friday, July 4, 2008 and the crew is busy putting the final touches on the incredible set up for tonight's event. Drew is supervising from the terrace when through the French doors comes his most honored and special guest, daughter Rebecca.

"So, what do you think. Should we do the fireworks during dessert or wait until later in the evening while everyone is dancing?" Drew looks around the pool area and then into the sky, obviously picturing his fireworks display to come later that evening.

Rebecca kisses her father on the cheek, "Whatever you think Daddy, it's always perfect. How does the time go so fast? I can't believe it is already 4th of July weekend again!"

"Just wait until you are my age, my dear. Then it really flies by. How about a cocktail with your old man?" He takes her hand and they walk into the house.

"That sounds fantastic. What are you in the mood for?"

"Why don't we open a real nice Bordeaux?" Drew asks for approval.

"Having you here all to myself for a few hours before the guests arrive makes me want to celebrate. I'll go to the wine cellar and pick one for us. In fact, someone gave me a very special bottle for my birthday this summer," winking at his daughter, "I've been saving it for just the two of us. Why don't you have Yvette put a little snack together and I'll meet you back here on the terrace in 20. We can catch up then. I want to hear all about your week. Especially want to talk to you about your business in this unstable banking environment."

"Perfect. I'd love to have some of your insight and advice. It is a volatile time, one I've never experienced in my years in IBK." Rebecca and Drew enter the house through the open French door into the study and go their separate ways into the house. Both excited about the evening like father and daughter on Christmas morning. Rebecca remembers all of the 4th of July parties at Morgan Manor ever since she was a young girl, always spectacular always memorable.

A true patriotic American, Drew Webb loves this day. He has served this country most of his adult life, trying to protect her from the threat of danger, a passion that will never leave him. He lives, eats and breaths his hope for a better America and his desire for perfect order. A country and a world where everything is just and right. From his early days as prosecutor to district court judge, the FBI and finally CIA, his heart and soul have been fully committed to working to help his beloved country achieve such order and for all things right for America and right for the world. He has been there, in the trenches through much history in the making. His fight against organized crime, his days in Washington where he saw the end of the Cold War, and that fateful day, September 11, 2001, the beginning of a new era. War on America's soil, something he always believed could possibly happen, but never believed it ever would. A true patriot, he still believes in the strength of his great country and after 911 his passion for her Independence Day grows even greater.

* * * * *

THE SUN HAS JUST SET IN NASSAU BAHAMAS, and the red sky seems to be on fire. Even the water has a deep red hue. Patric has never been so happy to be back on Mer Soleil as he is this evening. He reaches in his pocket and removes the memory card he had hidden. Sitting on the aft deck of the boat, he kisses the memory card and dials his friend Tim Connelly .

"Hey buddy, where are you?" Tim's voice is anxious on the other end of the phone.

"Nassau...on the boat. I'm going to fly back to the city tomorrow."

"Did you get anything?" an even more animated Tim is anxious to know the scoop.

"I've got some shots. I don't know exactly what I have, but I'll bring them up in my laptop tonight and see what's there. Hopefully I will have something good."

"How did it go down there?"

"A little hairy...not bad. I did lose the battery and a memory card in my camera to a Cuban police officer, otherwise, not so bad."

"What? Police?" Tim feels a pang deep in his stomach.

"No big deal, but whatever is going on at that place, nobody wants anyone to know about it. I've got a guy who may ask around for me, who knows. Probably won't get anything, but maybe someone will know something."

"You're amazing my friend. I wish I had more of your sense of adventure. Call me when you are back. I'll see you in the office Tuesday morning." Tim is obviously thrilled with the prospects.

"Let's not get too excited. I don't know if we have anything yet. We'll check it out when I get back. See you Tuesday." Patric disconnects the call and goes below deck to load the memory card on his laptop.

While Patric waits for the content of the memory card to download and appear on his computer screen, he turns on some tunes. An old Chris Isaak song comes up on the mix as an image has loaded on the laptop. He sits down zooming in and out. He explores the photos of the estate, the veranda, and the man sitting alone. Vaguely you can see what appears to be armed guards at the doorway. His cell phone rings. "Yeah." Patric answers.

"Amigo, this is Phillipe. I ask around about the house, este de playa. Nobody knows anything, but my cousin is a gardener, landscaper in the area and he said he thinks there is a witness protection deal in one of the mansions out there. Don't know if it is your mansion, but I told you I would call if I heard anything."

"Americans?" Patric asks.

"He doesn't know, but doesn't think so. Es solo herejia, heresay. Y no mucho. That is all I hear. No mas. Thanks for taking care of my brother in law. He said you gave him buen consejo...tip. Gracias."

"Gracias Phillipe. I really appreciate you checking it out for me."

"Si, placer. Hasta luego amigo."

"You take care of yourself." Patric puts down the phone and gets back to the computer.

"Witness protection?" Patric mutters aloud. "What is this shit all about?" He goes to the cooler and grabs a Heineken. Walking by the hatch he looks up into the sky. In the background, Chris Isaak's *Deep Blue Spanish Sky*, is playing, he sighs and smiles, how appropriate and how happy he is to be out of Cuba and back in familiar territory. Closing and locking the hatch, Patric goes on to resume in front of the computer screen. After this very long and somewhat harrowing day, the berth of Mer Soleil will feel like a feather bed at the St. Regis tonight. He will sleep like a rock.

THE EVENING COULDN'T BE MORE PERFECT, as the guests begin to arrive at Morgan Manor for the gala event of the summer. Rebecca greets guests as they make their entrance, most of whom she has grown up with, or have watched her grow up. Summers were wonderful coming up in this close knit community, she has such fond memories of each and every one.

"Hello, it is wonderful to see you." Rebecca greets an arriving couple.

"You look lovely Rebecca. Your father seems to be doing very well."

"I know. He keeps himself very busy."

"Have you met Leslie?" the woman asks almost gossipy.

"Yes, in fact, I met her over Memorial Day at Dad's birthday. She seems very nice. I just want him to be happy. It would be so nice for him to have someone special to spend time with. It has been so long since my mother is gone." Rebecca calms the inquiring tone.

"She is nice. We've had dinner with the two of them a few times. They seem to get on quite well together," the guest comments.

"That's great. Did you know her before?" Rebecca asks the couple.

"We knew of her, but not personally," she changes the subject. "We have some news. We are expecting another grandchild in the fall."

"Congratulations. You know Tim Connelly and his wife Maureen are expecting sometime this fall also." Rebecca mutters back.

"We've heard. They don't come out to the Hamptons like they did when you kids were younger."

"I know. It's easy to get wrapped up in the city, but I do try to get out here with Daddy as much as I can during the summer."

"He loves this house, it was their dream. Home means everything to him, it's really kind of special." Rebecca says as she looks around at all of the decorations, lights, candles and music. "Of course we've been listening to John Philip Sousa marches all afternoon!"

"You father is a character." They all laugh.

"Yes, that he is. Please have a drink and do pass my best wishes on to your daughter and son-in-law. Enjoy the evening." Rebecca steers them toward the bar and wanders toward the pool terrace picking up a glass of champagne from the waiter's tray as he walks through the crowd passing them around.

Drew and Leslie approach Rebecca hand in hand. Leslie looks stunning dawning a long gold lame' St. John knit gown. "Hey you two. Have you had a chance to dance?" Rebecca greets her father.

"Yes we have my darling. Can a tired old man have this dance with the prettiest girl at the party?" Drew asks of his daughter.

"Sounds like you have already been dancing with her." Rebecca smiles at Leslie who whispers back, "thank you."

"Come on Rebecca, let's shake a leg." Drew takes Rebecca's champagne glass and hands it to Leslie for safe keeping. "We'll be back in a few minutes." He winks at Leslie as he takes Rebecca to the pool terrace, aka dance floor.

As they dance Rebecca looks her father directly in the eye. "Leslie is lovely Daddy. I really like her…very much."

"She is great and we do enjoy each other's company. It is different, but I am having a very good time." Drew smiles.

"I think that is great, Daddy. Oh my goodness, Tim and Maureen just came out. I am so excited that they came." Rebecca sees the Connelly's make their way down the lawn to the pool terrace.

"You go enjoy your friends. I need to speak to someone. See you in a little while. Have fun princess!" Drew excuses himself and joins a group of men seeming to be in a very serious conversation. Rebecca notices the group, but is more intent on visiting with her dear friends.

"Hey you two. So glad you made it out! Maureen, you look fantastic. Are you feeling well?" Rebecca reaches for Maureen's hand. "And Timbo, I forgot how handsome you are in a tux!" The three friends embrace as the sound of fireworks begin.

The loud bang of the first dud gets everyone in the mood as the next moment a most beautiful display of sparkling light fills the sky. The crowd stops dancing and begins to applaud. Rebecca, Tim and Maureen walk toward the rest of the guests who now gather together poolside for the incredible show. Rebecca has always loved the fireworks, even as a young girl running to the edge of the property to get the best possible view. Though in those days, after the fireworks display, it was off to bed for the children as the adults would continue to party the night away. Yvette, always well prepared, with breakfast waiting for the night owls who turned into early birds in the early light of dawn.

The fabulous display of light seems to last for eternity as one after another, the sparkling lights of red, white and blue fill the clear black sky. The occasional gold swirly whistles it's way to the ground and draws an "ahhhh" from the crowd followed by more applause.

It is a beautiful evening and a beautiful party. Once again, The Honorable Drew Webb does not disappoint. It is the South Hampton event of the season.

* * * * *

CHAPTER TEN

IT IS EARLY MORNING AND AS THE SUN RISES OVER THE CITY, the fluorescent light of the night gives way to the natural sunlight marking the beginning of a new day. The New York Times newsroom is buzzing with the headlines of the day as well as the long holiday weekend social scoop. Patric Taylor, still lagging just a bit from his trip, walks into Tim Connelly's office, red weary eyed, Starbucks in hand.

"Welcome back. So, what have you got?"

"Good morning to you too." Patric takes his briefcase off of his shoulder and puts it in one of Tim's office chairs, while taking a seat in the other. "I think I got some great shots."

"Bring 'em on brother."

"Patience my friend." Patric is moving a bit slowly this morning as he pulls his laptop out of his bag. He sets it up on Tim's desk and loads the shots, bringing up the first aerial.

"Quite a place. Did you ever hear anything more about what is going on there?" Tim is a little disappointed with the pics so far.

"Not exactly, but the rumor from a landscaper in the area is that it is a witness protection property. They don't think it is Americans though."

"What do you think?" Tim has his own ideas and by this time definitely thinks it is related in some way to the Cuba situation press conference but they need more info., much more.

"I don't know, but I am certain that the guy at the press conference was the same guy at this place the last time I photographed it."

"So, he was not there this time?" Tim asks, still disappointed as they continue to click through the photographs on Patric's laptop.

"No, but someone was. Check this one out." Patric frames the photo on the screen of the gentleman sitting alone on the veranda and zooms in as much as possible before the screen becomes too blurry.

"Holy Mother of God! Patric, do you think that could be…? I think it might be a good time to get Weller involved. Let's see what he thinks about it." Tim looks up at his friend. "He was at the Webb's place this weekend…" before Tim could finish his sentence Patric interjects.

"Right…the annual 4th of July bash. Great party if you like to bull shit with a bunch of people who think what they think matters." Patric comments, less than respectfully and very cynically.

"Weller wasn't the only heavy hitter at the party and I noticed the lot of them in what appeared to be a very deep conversation. And Patric, not everyone in South Hampton is superficial."

"Most everyone. Well, it is an election year. I am sure these guys are doing some heavy politicking and positioning about now."

"Stop being so judgmental man. I grew up there too you know and Becca's family has always been first rate. Drew Webb is a good man." Tim defends his roots and the Webb's.

"He never liked me very much." Patric adds.

"He just didn't get to know you. Besides, all fathers are exceptionally protective when it comes to their daughters. My kid isn't even here yet and I am already protective about everything, even simple, insignificant decisions for the future." Tim pauses as he looks back at the computer screen. "I've got willies in my stomach. I'm getting us a meeting with Weller."

Tim picks up his office phone and dials an extension. "Is he available? Thanks." There is a pause. "Good afternoon sir…fine thanks."

"Yes, it was a great party. Do you have a minute? Patric Taylor is here and he has taken some shots that I think could be pertinent. I'd like for you to take a look." There is another pause while Times Editor Bill Weller responds to Tim. "I'd rather explain in person. Thank you sir." Tim hangs up the phone and looks up at Patric.

"He's on his way. PT, do you think that's really fuckin' bin Laden?"

"I can't believe you picked up on that right away. It took me hours of looking and re-looking, analyzing and re-analyzing. I guess I just didn't want to over react, or even believe what I might have gotten."

"I think you got it alright partner...and if it is what we think and who we think it is, obviously someone in Washington is right in the middle of it. What the fuck?" Tim is getting excited. His palms are beginning to sweat and he is frothing at the mouth like any other good reporter who may have just landed something big...the big story he was destined to write and before anyone else has so much as an inkling. But where is this story going? It is only a hunch with much work to be done, but it appears to be a once in a lifetime opportunity.

"I'm just thinking out loud here, but Gitmo is only a diversion here. It's not that they don't want any media at Gitmo, they don't want anyone finding what you found. What are the chances?" Tim looks one more time at the computer screen on his desk. "Shit Patric, if you really saw Becca's new client at this place, I am worried about her. This guy could be dangerous."

Bill Weller abruptly walks into the office. "Okay, what have you boys got?" He shakes their hands quickly and Tim points toward the computer screen. "Where was this taken?"

"Patric took it in Cuba last weekend, sir." Tim gets up from his chair and invites Bill Weller to walk around the desk and take a seat. "It sounds crazy, I know, but we believe the man in the photograph to be, well, bin Laden, sir. I know it's far fetched, but the resemblance."

"It's pretty close." Weller puts on his reading glasses and leans very close to the screen. "Patric what were you doing in Cuba?"

"I was there on vacation a few months ago and stumbled across this place while doing some free lance work. Anyway, I took a few shots from a hillside not far from the property. Then after Tim and I went to the press conference in DC the following week, which consequently was addressing the Cuba issue, I saw a man there that I was certain was in the original photographs that I had taken at this place. I didn't think about it at first, but when the Cuban issue was discussed at the press conference and the fact that the government wanted the press off of Guantanamo and out of Cuba, I went home and reviewed the shots that I had taken there. It was obvious something was going on at this estate with the posted guards and everything, and when I zoomed in on the entrance, I had a shot of a gentleman leaving the place who looked very close to the guy we saw standing in the back of the room at the conference. It just seemed too coincidental at the time, so I went back down this past weekend to see what I could find out which is when I was able to take the aerials."

"Besides the photographs, do you two have any other information?" Weller is so far not impressed, and they know it. He clicks through the rest of the photographs in the file.

"No sir. Only second hand hearsay, apparently from a landscaper in the area who says the property is being used as a witness protection safe house. It is obviously well guarded." Tim responds.

"Taylor, how the hell did you get these photos and how the hell did you get out of Cuba with them?" Weller takes his readers off, puts them on the desk and looks directly at Patric.

"It's a long boring story sir, but I did hide the memory card to get it out of the country." Somewhat cavalier, Patric answers Weller.

"Authorities did take some of his equipment though." Tim interjects.

"Do we have enough to start to investigate further?" Tim continues.

"What kind of story are you thinking about, Tim? Right now you have nothing. Some Cuban here say and some photos of a guy at what appears to be a guarded estate, somewhere in the world, you say Cuba, where someone who somewhat resembles the greatest terror threat to the United States and to the world just happens to be residing. For all we know it could just be some wealthy Arab on vacation at his oceanfront Cuban estate. Most of those oil guys carry a staff of bodyguards with them just about everywhere. From where I am sitting, you have nothing." Weller cautious and still unimpressed.

"I know it's far fetched, but could we continue to pursue it? Just on the outside chance that it is bin Laden, and all of this is somehow related to our government and that press conference. This is an election year sir, and the man that we saw at the press conference, and we believe Patric saw in Cuba, definitely ties our country to whatever is going on down there. One can only speculate, I know, but we have a line on this guy. I realize that it is totally speculative." Tim trying to plead his case for further investigation.

"Speculation is what gets newspapers sued and puts people like us out of business or worse. This is a very sensitive issue Tim, we can't afford to take chances with the small, even trite, amount of information that you think you have." Weller pauses. "What do you mean you have a line on this guy?"

"Well, believe it or not, I've seen this guy on one other occasion here in New York. He is a new client of Rebecca Webb's. She gave me his business card. We tried following up on that and research can't find anything on him based on the business card anyway. It is as if he doesn't really exist." Tim is on a roll now and he has his editor's attention.

"Drew Webb's daughter, Rebecca?" Weller asks very slowly.

Weller gets up from the desk and walks toward the door. He turns around, "Okay gentlemen. Before I ask you to give this up permanently, there is someone I want you to talk to about what little information you do have. And I want you to share the photos with him as well."

"Who would that be sir?" Patric asks, even though he already knows exactly who Bill Weller is inferring.

"Drew Webb. He has a lot of secured information about the Cuban issue and I think he would find these photos of interest. I'm not giving the green light to pursue this, I'm just saying you have my permission to meet with Webb and get his thoughts. Tim, I will give him a call and arrange a meeting for you to review your suspicions with him. If he can put the pieces to the puzzle together and give you something to go on, you may pursue this further. If not, I don't see that you have anything here except a few coincidences and I am not going to hang this newspaper out to dry based on that."

"I understand, thank you sir. But what does Drew Webb have to do with current secured information, and with all due respect, how do you know about that?" Tim knows now that they are on to something and knows that his editor knows it too. If Drew Webb will be able to share any information it could just be the catalyst to really get this story going.

"I don't know much Tim, and this conversation does not leave this room." Weller looks at both gentlemen and waits for a positive confirmation from each of them. "Is that understood?" They both nod. "I know that there is a very powerful group of people concerned about covert efforts to affect the upcoming election. There has been talk about the possibility of someone being aware of the whereabouts of Osama bin Laden and other key al Quaeda leaders and this would, of course have tremendous impact on upcoming elections. Drew Webb is your man. I'll get the meeting, you get your ducks in a row."

Weller picks his glasses up off of Tim's desk, walks out of the office and closes the door behind him.

"This thing is getting too close to home bro. I've heard of the small world phenomenon, six degrees and all of that bull shit, but this is scary." Patric is even more convinced now that these events though shallow in proof, and highly circumstantial, are no coincidence. He feels his stomach cramp and takes a deep breath.

"No shit. We'll see what Drew Webb has to say when Weller gets our meeting. Do you think Becca could be involved in this somehow?" Tim is thinking out loud and seems concerned himself.

"If she is, she has no idea. She doesn't have a clue, but I'm willing to bet that her new client Mr. Zandieh, knows exactly who her father is." Patric 's throat is dry and his palms are sweating. He feels his face turning white as he now mentally concludes that Rebecca's new client and possible love interest is interested in more than investment advice and more than a romantic trist with his ex.

Tim notices his friend's anguish and knows that it is not just the ex-boyfriend jealousy syndrome. "Amen to that brother."

* * * * *

ON THE OTHER SIDE OF MANHATTAN, a busy Rebecca Webb leans toward her computer screen shaking her head as she watches the numbers. She has always been good at predicting the markets and understanding the daily flow. This summer has been different. There is something in the wings, something volatile. Even her close contacts on the inside of the trading floor are dumbfounded. The sub prime market is a disaster and bank stocks are dropping with little recovery. Rebecca rests her chin on the back of her hand, supported by her elbow on the desk. She sighs deeply. This business is not fun anymore she thinks. What happened to the fun days of trading, investing and advising. They weren't that long ago. Now, there seems to be no end in sight to this stressful, instability. She feels the tremendous weight of people entrusting her with their hard earned and accumulated wealth and good fortune. Today, she is just trying to hold on to it for them and protect their positions.

The stress is taking its toll and Rebecca is exhausted, almost depressed. The hours seem to fly by, though she accomplishes very little. As she continues to stare at the screen, a text message chimes on her phone and startles her. Rebecca picks up the phone to reply. It reads, "*Is this my investment counselor?*" It is the London cell phone number of Geoffrey Zandieh. Rebecca welcomes the break from her computer screen, and even more so, needed one.

"*Hi. How is your day?*" She puts the phone down on her desk and waits for his reply.

"*Somewhat productive. How was your party?*" He responds.

"*Party was lovely. My father really knows how to do it right. You still on the other side of the pond?*" She hits send and this time keeps the phone in her hand as she watches her I phone screen for the reply.

"*Yes. I am still in London. Did you receive your itinerary for the weekend?*" Rebecca did receive the information, but does not respond. She knows it is time to make a decision one way or another.

She puts the phone back down on the desk and leans back in her chair. There is a part of her that really wants to go to the Ocean Club, another part of her that really wants...needs to get away. But something continues to cause hesitation. What is it, why can't I just make a decision, she thinks to herself. Taking another deep breath she turns and looks out the window towards the river. The continuous flow of the water usually clears her mind and when deliberating on a difficult business decision, it helps bring her to a conclusion. She relies on her view quite often for support and direction and once again she looks down to the water for a solution.

The phone chimes again. She turns back to her desk and looks at the message. *"You are still joining me in the Bahamas, aren't you?"*

She responds instantaneously almost without thought, *"I'd love to but..."* Surely he will get the message, she thinks, then says aloud, "How the hell will he get the message when I don't even know what I want to do."

The chime rings again. It appears Mr. Zandieh does not want to take no for an answer. *"No excuses. You deserve a weekend away and I have already told you there is absolutely no pressure. I've reserved a fantastic suite for you at the Ocean Club, all to yourself. Come. Have a good time."*

She doesn't respond right away and again looks out to the river for advice. Again, a chime. *"I think you might like me if you got to know me better. Perhaps that is what you are afraid of."*

Now Rebecca is laughing out loud. He is right, she does need a break and she is putting much too much pressure on herself about a simple decision to get away for a few days. *"Who said I was afraid? I am just very busy here right now,"* she responds back. This little challenge is now beginning to be fun and Geoffrey Zandieh knows he just hooked his catch.

"All the more reason for a weekend away." He texts back. He, too, loves this bantering about and he knows she loves the challenge as much as he.

"You drive a hard bargain Mr. Zandieh." Rebecca types and starts to push, send, but something causes her again to hesitate. What is wrong with me? This is ridiculous, she thinks to herself. She feels giddy all of a sudden, like a young school girl playing hard to get for a prom date. She hits send and drops the phone down on the desk, pulling her hand back as if it were too hot to touch.

"Ah, I've got her, hook line and sinker." He thinks aloud, then types. *"I've made all the arrangements and I promise to give you as much time to yourself as you need."* There is almost a sense a relief.

She is laughing out loud once again. *"Ok...ok...stop already. I'll see you Friday afternoon in Paradise."* She hits send and puts the phone down on her desk for the last time. A message immediately comes back, *"Splendid."* and this text session is over.

Of course she has second thoughts. "What am I thinking? What is he thinking?" She ponders for one moment more. "Oh well, it is done, now I can get excited at the thought of a wonderful weekend at the Ocean Club." Rebecca turns her attention back to the screen as if she didn't miss a tick. The markets are still bouncing around like children on a trampoline, and so is Rebecca's stomach. Was it something she had for lunch or is it just this crazy market? Perhaps it could be her impending trip with one Geoffrey Zandieh.

None are relevant at the moment and her business mind re-focuses on the matter at hand. Quite knowingly, she is prepared to work very hard, long hours this week to diligently wrap up all of the files on her cluttered desk. Though it seems impossible at this moment that she will feel good about a few days away from it, she will relish and enjoy her much deserved and needed mini-vacation to the beautiful and pristine Ocean Club.

IT IS TEN O'CLOCK PM IN LONDON AS THE SKY begins to turn black and the stars rise over the capital of Great Britain. The lights of the city are beautiful from Geoffrey Zandieh's office in Knightsbridge. It's a lovely summer evening and Zandieh will sleep very well tonight knowing that the next segment of this operation is underway and that the entire operation is nearly complete. He pulls the draperies back and peers out the window. The city lights illuminate the quite devious, almost scary grin on his face, which transitions into a soft smile. With a look of perplexity, he thinks aloud. "Sweet Rebecca Webb, what will become of her? Do I even have a remote chance with this amazing woman after this deal is behind me?" Though rather wishful and most unlikely, he thinks about a time with her some time in the future. A day when he will have plenty of resources, more than enough time and a clear conscience. A time that he might dream of spending with Rebecca Webb in much different circumstances. A time for explanation and, hopefully, forgiveness. A time for a new and wonderful adventure in his life. A time for love.

Geoffrey reaches in his pocket for his cell phone. Placing a call he puts the phone to his ear, still peering out the window over London town. "It has been arranged. (pause) I understand."

* * * * *

CHAPTER ELEVEN

CENTRAL PARK IS BUZZING THIS MORNING with the usual morning runners and walkers, tourists and street vendors. For a mid July day, it is actually quite lovely. The sky is deep blue, the humidity is low, a perfect morning to shoot for the cover of New York Magazine. Patric loves the light at this time of the morning and is a master at using it in his portrait and landscape photography. The morning glare resonates through the trees in the park and reflects the ripples of water swimming across the pond in the breeze. He experiments with the angles of light through the lens of his camera and directs the staff to move parts of the set to correspond to the lighting. Taking a short break to have a sip of coffee, he notices a text message on his phone. *"We've got a meeting with Webb Friday afternoon at his office here in the city. 4:00."* Patric pushes the call back on the message and rings Tim Connelly's cell.

"You get my text?" Tim answers. "Weller called last night and said that Drew Webb was coming into the city Friday morning for some business, so he will meet with us at 4:00 that afternoon."

"Does he know what it is about?" Patric is curious and especially curious of Drew Webb's reaction to a meeting with him.

"Weller filled him in on our meeting. He said Webb is interested in seeing the shots from Cuba."

"Does he know who took them?" Patric can't help but ask.

"Yes, and according to Bill, Webb even sends you his regards."

"Easy for him to say now that I am not in his daughter's life any longer. He couldn't see us sooner than Friday?" Patric's voice turns anxious. He can't control the pang of anxiety in his stomach and wonders if it is because of Rebecca or just the meeting with her father.

"Dude, stop worrying about insignificant shit and let's get ready for this meeting. We've got something Patty my boy I know it. Something big and Drew Webb is going to help us break the biggest story our country has seen since 911." Tim is anxious also, but excitedly so. He feels it, he just knows that they are going to get something from Drew Webb, something that will lead them right into his big story, the story of his lifetime.

"You are right on there my friend. Friday at 4 it is." Patric disconnects, puts the phone in the leg pocket of his cargo pants and gets back to the photo shoot.

Every publication in Manhattan wants the gifted and talented Patric Taylor to shoot their covers and he appreciates being sought after. He is masterful, creative, professional and works very fast, using natural resources such as light as a Henri Rousseau, Edouard Manet or Claude Monet would do, by creating light with dramatic brushstrokes. This business is his bread and butter and he knows he is the best.

Timing is money, and the timing couldn't be more perfect at this moment. Patric organizes and arranges the models as he begins to create his masterpiece taking many shots from many angles. He is moving quickly taking advantage of the moment as the sweat begins to form droplets on his forehead and run like cool water down the side of his chiseled face. His long, wavy, dark hair also begins to drip with the perspiration as he wipes his forehead with a towel. Patric is keyed up, invigorated. His senses can feel the essence of developing great material. Not always what the customer thinks they are looking for...but even better.

His work here is done.

* * * * *

A BLACK CADILLAC LIMOSUINE WAITS PATIENTLY in front of 2 East 70th as Rebecca walks swiftly out of the elevator and through the front doors of the building. The driver waits car-side with the rear passenger door open, under the shade of the green awning that joins the front of the building to the hot black street. The sun is shining brightly and there is a blinding glare reflecting off of the black limo into Rebecca's line of sight. She is approached by the driver who reaches for her Louis Vuitton Pegase rolling bag, "Good Morning. Miss Webb?"

"Yes, thank you." Rebecca hands the bag over to the driver and takes her seat in the back of the limo. The car has been left running and the cool air conditioning gives her a chill, straight up her spine. The question, or the idea of, whether or not this trip is a good idea has left her conscious thoughts, perhaps prematurely. With a deep sigh, she pushes her white Chanel sunglasses to rest above her forehead pulling her beautiful summer blonde hair back off of her face. She fumbles through her handbag for her phone. Dressed for summer in the islands in a beautiful white spaghetti strap Missoni dress and white bejeweled Havianas, she is crisply beautiful, ready to get away and really looking forward to seeing the tiffany blue water of the Bahamas.

The driver slams the trunk closed and comes around to also close the passenger door peeking in at his passenger. "To Laguradia?" He asks. Rebecca nods. "Is there anything that I can get for you?" She notices his heavily scented cologne and how hot he must be in his finely tailored black suit, heavily starched white linen shirt and tie.

"I'm fine, thank you," she responds kindly to the driver. He closes her door and walks around the outside of the limousine watching for traffic from behind as he enters the car.

Turning back to her he adds, "The traffic is a bit heavy this morning but I will get you to the airport as quickly as possible."

With that, the driver puts the car in gear and they are off to Laguardia. Rebecca leans back to get comfortable in the cushy black leather seat and dials her iPhone, reaching Maggie's voice mail.

"Hey Mag, it's me. I'm on my way to the airport. John, my doorman has a key for you to get into the apartment. Make yourself at home and call me on my cell if you need anything. I'll see you Sunday night. Have a great weekend. Love ya. Byeeeeee..." She puts the phone back into her bag, puts her head back to rest on the seat and rolls it to the side to take in the view of the Manhattan skyline as the car leaves the city. Though it had been a very mild week, the haze is back filtering the deep blue sky until it looks almost white. It will be a hot day in the city.

She must have dozed off and is startled when the driver is asking which airline she will be flying today. Her heart is pounding very quickly as if it is going to jump out of her chest and a piercing anxiety takes over her body. Taking a few deep breaths to calm herself, she refreshes her lip stick as the driver comes around to let her out of the car. He opens the door and the hot air from outside hits her in the face, like she has just opened a hot oven door. She takes her handbag and gets out of the car. Pulling her sunglasses back down over her eyes, Rebecca hands the driver his fee as he hands her the pull handle of her bag. As she enters the airport, everyone turns to watch this lovely presence walk past, she is stunningly chic, a tall cool glass of water on a hot summer's day. Rebecca strolls through the airport quickly and efficiently through the first class check-in, security and by the time she arrives at the gate, the agent has already begun the boarding process. "What great timing," she thinks to herself.

The first class cabin is already full except for Rebecca's seat. She stops to be seated. The attractive man in the aisle seat next to hers stands to hand his suit jacket to the flight attendant then turns to help Rebecca stow her rolling bag in the overhead bin. "Thank you." She smiles, thanking the man for his assistance.

"My pleasure," responds the man. Rebecca takes her seat on the window and places her handbag under the seat in front of her. She can't help but notice him. A professional athlete at one time perhaps, or so it would seem. He is dressed casually but slightly elegant for a man of his stature, Armani-esque navy suit and crisp, white button down shirt. She feels him also looking toward her, wondering who is this lovely lady who has been seated to his right for the trip to parts south.

"Are you traveling to Nassau for business or pleasure?" He turns to Rebecca.

She giggles, "You know, I am not completely sure. And you?"

"I am going to the Ocean Club to play golf with a friend of mine who has a home there. Your trip sounds interesting." He also breaks a chuckle as he settles back into his seat. The flight attendant is passing through the first class cabin and asks the two if they would care for something to drink before take off.

"A bottle of water please, no ice. Thank you." Rebecca leans toward the window and watches the ground crew scurry about loading the last of the luggage preparing the plane to leave the departure area.

"Gin and tonic for me please." The man fumbles with some paper in his briefcase for just a moment, then closes and slides it under the seat. He sits back and closes his eyes, but only for a moment when the flight attendant returns with their drinks.

"Thank you." Rebecca reaches across the man for her water and the flight attendant gently sits the gin and tonic on the center console. The effervescence from the cocktail tingles Rebecca's arm. "It's a great golf course...the Ocean Club. You will enjoy it." She makes idle conversation.

The man looks at her while he picks up his still fizzing drink. "So, you've played it before?" He takes a sip.

"A time or two. My family used to have a home at Ocean Club Estates, but when we lost my mother some years ago, my father sold the house. We are still members there, though I haven't been back."

"I'm sorry," the man responds compassionately.

"Oh, thanks. It's okay really. She was very ill. It just killed my father, but he is doing great now. By the way, Rebecca Webb." She reaches over with her right hand to shake with her seatmate.

"Pleased to meet you Rebecca Webb, Ty Jones." The flight attendant interrupts to collect Mr. Jones' glass for take off. "That was fast." He obviously wasn't quite ready to give up his cocktail. "I've not played the course as yet. I have been down to gamble at the Atlantis but the new golf course wasn't open as yet at that time. I am looking forward to playing."

"It is really beautiful, I think you will like what Weiskopf did with the property. Pretty much every hole has a view of the ocean."

"You sound like you are a good golfer, what's your handicap?"

"It's been a while since I played on a regular basis, but when I was younger and played quite a bit I carried around an 18-20 at one time. It didn't last long though, once I started working a lot I didn't have as much time to spend on the golf course." Rebecca chuckles.

"You need to get back out there and play. Will you be playing this weekend?" He turns to her as the plane begins to push back and taxi toward the runway. It is just about 2 hours from Laguardia to Nassau over the blue waters of the Atlantic the entire way.

Rebecca loved the family competition of playing golf with her father and brother. He was an outstanding athlete, and exceptional golfer. She peers out the window and thinks of those fun days when her brother was still alive. "I'm not really sure what I am doing this trip, probably just relaxing in the sun."

113

"I've had a few very stressful weeks in my business, so I am really looking forward to just watching the surf and soaking in the sun. Where do you play your golf in New York?"

"I spend most of my time on the coast actually, left coast. I was just passing through the city for some business. I used to live here, but moved out west when I officially retired."

"LA?" She asks, the gentleman nods. "I love LA, great city. I am just a New York City girl...it is home."

"So you grew up in the city?" He seems surprised.

"Long Island mostly, South Hampton. My father worked in the city and I ended up going to school in New York and starting my career here, so I guess I am pretty much planted now." Her New York City girl pride shines through.

The captain interrupts to announce that their flight is ready for takeoff. Rebecca has enjoyed visiting with Mr. Ty Jones, whoever he is. Though he never did mention what it was that he retired from, she felt almost embarrassed, as though she should know who he is, and she felt fairly certain that he thought she did. Funny actually, though being someone who follows sports fairly well, and New York City sports very well, his name still didn't ring a bell.

"Well, enjoy your weekend. I think I better catch a nap before a busy weekend." Jones leans back and closes his eyes, hands folded on his lap.

Rebecca turns her attention out the window once again taking in each moment of take off. She gets so excited by the feeling of being thrown back in the seat, just a little, when the thrusters release and again when the wheels under the nose lift off the ground. Taking in the view, she notices the haze surrounding the city skyline, though sunlight still reflects the glare from the tall buildings.

There is almost a halo over the city as the plane ascends above the low stratospheric clouds and into the deep blue sky above. Dozing off into a light sleep, Rebecca dreams of the days as a young girl on vacation in the Bahamas and later with Patric sailing on the Mer Soleil. She dreams of friends on the island and the beautiful home that her father built for her mother for a special birthday in the Ocean Club Estates. It was going to be their retirement home, their dream to live at the Ocean Club home and spend summers back in South Hampton. The best of both worlds they thought. Their dream was just becoming reality when Rebecca's mother became ill.

As the plane begins to descend over the beautiful blue water, 1,000 shades of Bahamian blue, and toward Linden Pindling International Airport, Rebecca opens her eyes, taking in every bit of the incredible reflection of light from the sun through the water to the reefs below.

Boats are sailing on this particularly calm day and as the plane makes a low left turn toward final descent, a sharp ray of sunlight pierces the water below in a bright flash. She feels as if she were coming home, home to a special and beloved place and realizes in this moment how much she has missed it here. She pictures herself on the veranda at her parent's home, taking in the vast view of the ocean and running as fast as she can through the granular sand beach to dive into the warm turquoise water. Wonderful memories of beautiful days that went away all too quickly, perhaps taken for granted, but always appreciated and eternally revered.

* * * * *

TWO MOST DETERMINED GENTLEMEN and lifelong pals make their way into the law offices of Rooney, Stein, Rosen, and Webb, P.A., a beautiful upper east side brownstone turned law office in the late 1950's. Drew Webb loved this law firm, his first law partnership after leaving the New York District Court Post. He was honored to be asked to join as a partner in such a respected firm and they were honored to have him. As a young prosecuting attorney, Drew Webb was known as an incredible litigator and later as an honest, fair and discerning Judge, of utmost integrity. Though Drew doesn't practice much in these later days, he loves coming into to the city and working in his office. His Washington connections keep him in the game, and he thrives on this involvement.

"We've got everything together, right?" Tim turns to Patric as they stand at the reception desk.

Patric nods as the receptionist looks up at the two sharply dressed young men. "Drew Webb, please. Tim Connelley and Patric Taylor. He is expecting us." Tim announces.

"Take a seat gentlemen. I'll let Judge Webb know that you are here."

Tim and Patric sit down on a long cushy leather sofa in the reception area. A typical law office. Deep rich colors, antique furnishings, heavy paisley draperies tied back on the large window paned windows. "Dude, let's have a beer after this. It's been a long day, long week. Mo is so hormonal, I can't wait to have this baby."

"I'm up for a cold one. I've got no plans tonight." Patric appeases his friend.

"What, no hot date tonight? Friday night in the city and the handsome, eligible Patric Taylor has no plans?" Tim teases.

"No man. It's just me and the Yankees on the tube tonight." Patric justifies his empty dance card for the evening.

"What happened to that underfed model you were hanging out with?"

"I still see her now and again. Nice girl." Patric humbly replies.

"She's hot, a real looker. Maybe she's into baseball on a Friday night."

"Thanks, bud, but I can tree my own dates. You're welcome to join me for the game if Maureen is cool with it." Patric looks up at the receptionist who is making eye contact.

"Gentlemen, Judge Webb will see you now. Down the hall to your right all the way to the end of the hallway. You'll see his office just in front of you."

Tim and Patric rise from the sofa and start that way. "Thank you." Patric says as he smiles and nods at the very pretty young lady. She smiles back in a sweet, demure sort of way bowing her head yet maintaining eye contact, as if to be shy.

"You are such a dog man. How do you do it?" Tim gives his friend a dig and a firm pat on the ass, though thoroughly enjoying watching the affect his pal Patric has on the ladies...and totally unintentional. As they make their way to the end of the paneled hallway, Drew Webb is waiting for them outside his office doorway.

"Please, come in." Webb reaches out and shakes both gentleman's hands and guides the way into his office by pointing with his left arm.

"Thank you sir. Nice to see you again." Tim passes by Webb into the office and Patric follows. Webb closes the door behind him and comes into the office himself. The office is spacious with high molded ceilings. A large crystal chandelier hangs from the center and the walls are lined with mahogany shelves, filled with books and law journals. Webb directs the gentlemen to a conversation area with sofa and club chairs. The coffee table is covered in a selection of today's newspapers and the most current business and political magazines.

"Tim, how is your lovely wife feeling? This must be an exciting time for you two." The Judge makes small talk, but is sincere.

"She is fine sir. Just waiting for the big day." Tim, ever the proud father to be , leans back into his chair.

"I remember waiting for our first...Rebecca. Her mother was so beautiful. We couldn't wait to be parents. What are you up to these days Patric? I have seen some of your recent work. I must say, quite impressive."

"Thank you sir. I appreciate that. I have been given some incredible opportunities the past few years." Patric responds in his usual humble manner. He is uncontrollably nervous, palms moist with sweat, his heart pounding. "This is ridiculous," he thinks to himself. Only in the presence of Drew Webb does he feel so inferior. Maybe he wasn't good enough for The Honorable Judge Drew Webb's most perfect daughter, but after all of these years, he still gets under Patric's skin. It isn't that Patric doesn't respect him, or even that he doesn't like him, because he does actually, very much on both counts. It is just the unfair sentiment of being felt unworthy, not quite good enough, just not the right one for the greatest love of his life.

"I have seen some of your magazine work, but I was actually speaking of your artistic pieces. Rebecca has shown me several. She is quite taken by the Central Park series that you did." Webb reveals.

"Rebecca has some of my pieces?" Patric is a bit taken back. He knows exactly what pieces Webb is referring to which were shown in a gallery for some time. He remembers getting the call from the gallery owner asking if he would sell. A local collector was interested in them for their home and was offering a very good price, he was told.

"I assumed she got them from you. Anyway, back to why you two are here today, what have you got for me. Bill Weller mentioned some photos from Cuba?" Webb gets back to the matter at hand.

Tim reaches inside his briefcase and pulls from it a large manila envelope and hands it to Webb. "Bill said that you may be working on something that could possibly be related."

Webb opens the envelope and shuffles through the photographs. "Oh my God. Gentlemen, if these photographs represent what it appears they may, you may have stumbled upon one of the greatest political scandals of the modern era." Still leafing through the photos, he holds one up with Zandieh leaving the Cuban estate. "Where were these taken Patric?"

"Just outside of Havana sir. I stumbled upon the estate by accident and took some shots. What interested me enough to go back for more is that we are fairly sure that the gentleman in that photograph was also present at a press conference in DC that Tim was covering for the Times, regarding the Guantanamo Bay issue, in essence to call the media off of Guantanamo."

"Can you be certain that this gentleman was at that press conference?" Webb looks at both men with a long and serious glance.

"We believe so sir, though we can't be certain since the photograph is a bit grainy. But what is even more interesting," Tim pauses and looks toward Patric for approval. Patric nods affirmatively and Tim continues, "I don't quite know how to say this sir without seeming a bit absurd, but we believe that he may also be a new client that Rebecca is working with from London."

"Do you have any information about him? Have you spoken with Rebecca about it?" Webb's voice is obviously showing signs of concern. This is getting too close, too convenient. He spent most of his years as a prosecutor, Judge and Washington intelligence head, protecting his family from just such a threat. How could he have been so careless this time? The heat was on and he knew it. How could he allow this situation to get so close to the most important person in the world to him, his beloved daughter, Rebecca.

"Yes, sir. We did speak with Becca. His name is Geoffrey Zandieh." Tim hands Webb the business card that Rebecca gave him. "She didn't really know anything about him. She said he came to her by referral, from someone here, in your firm. He needed an international investment banker to handle his portfolio and Rebecca came highly recommended."

"Sir," Patric interjects, "Tim and I don't think it is a coincidence that he happened to seek Rebecca's expertise."

"Surely you ran a background on the guy, Tim? Anything there?"

"Basically sir, the guy doesn't exist. At least not through any method of research that I have access to." Tim responds.

Webb holds his index finger up as to say "just a moment" and presses the intercom button on the telephone on the end table next to his chair. A female voice answers, "Yes Judge Webb?"

"Susan, get my daughter on the phone please. Thanks." Webb turns back to Tim and Patric. "No gentlemen, I don't think my daughter's new client is a coincidence either." There is a buzz on the intercom.

"Yes Susan, do you have Rebecca on the line?"

"So sorry. I spoke with her assistant and she is not in the office today. I tried her cell phone, but it went immediately into voice mail. I did leave her a message to call you as soon as possible. Would you like me to try her apartment?"

"Yes Susan, if you would please. Thanks."

The office get's quiet. All three men look at each other somewhat anxiously. Webb gets up and walks very quickly to his desk looking for his cell phone which he finds in his top desk drawer. Returning to his chair next to Tim and Patric, he begins to dial his phone as another buzz comes through on the intercom. "Yes, Susan."

"I reached a friend of Rebecca's who answered at her apartment, Maggie?" She apparently is staying there this weekend and mentioned that Rebecca is on her way to the Bahamas for the weekend with a new client. Do you want me to keep trying her cell?"

"No, thanks Susan. I will try myself." He dials Rebecca's number which goes immediately to voice mail. "Rebecca honey, it's Dad, please give me a call as soon as you get this message. It's important." Webb puts the phone down in his lap and rubs his temples with both hands looking at the floor. He looks up. "Gentlemen, I can't go into exactly what this is all about at the moment, but I assure you, when we have enough evidence and it is time to expose this deal, Tim, you will be the man handling the story. In the meantime, we need to find my daughter. Can you help me?" Both men nod. "I'll need to hang on to these photographs for the time being. Patric, do you still keep a boat in Nassau?"

"Yes sir, I do."

"I'm going to find out exactly where Rebecca is supposed to be and could I ask you to get down there and help me bring my daughter home? Of course, I will take care of any expense."

"Absolutely, it would be my pleasure, sir. I am sure she is fine. Rebecca Webb is a strong woman." Patric tries to ease Webb's mind, but he knows the situation is not good. For the Honorable Drew Webb to be visibly concerned is just as much concerning and worrisome to Patric and Tim as it obviously is to Rebecca's father.

"Tim, he may need your help down there. Could you get away for a short period of time? I would be most grateful. I know my daughter considers the two of you among her closest and best friends in the world. Make any arrangements through Susan and I will be in touch. Make sure she has all of your contact information, cell phone numbers and so on, before you leave." Webb takes a long deep breath and exhales slowly.

Webb stands, visibly shaken, "Guys, we can't trust anyone with this right now and time is of the essence. Do I have your commitment to keeping a lid on this until I can come up with some answers and we are able to locate Rebecca?"

"Yes sir, of course sir." Both men nod as they also rise to shake hands with Webb once again.

"I will brief Susan on your way to her office. She is three doors down on the left. I'll be in touch. If you will excuse me, I have a few urgent calls to make. Thanks, gentlemen." Webb leads Tim and Patric to the door of his office and directs them to Susan's office. He turns back into his office and closes the door behind him. By the time Tim and Patric reach Susan, Drew is already on the intercom giving Susan instructions on how to proceed in making some arrangements for them. His voice quivers as he explains the situation to her and she too turns a pale shade of gray only exaggerated by the fluorescent lighting coming from her office ceiling. Susan calmly, but with a sternly serious look about her, motions for the two gentlemen to approach her desk as she quickly punches the keys on her computer. Her acrylic fingernails tapping every key as if to be sending a morse code message.

"Shit. This is a little surreal for me, man." Tim whispers to his friend.

"Unfuckingbelievable." Patric whispers back as they approach Susan's desk.

"What the hell are we going to do?" Tim also looks a bit faint in the fluorescent light.

"I think we are going to the Bahamas, my friend."

"Shit, I can't go to the Bahamas. I've got a pregnant, hormonal wife who needs a husband and a baby on the way who needs a father. This thing is too big for us." Tim is in a panic, knowing he has no choice.

"Do you want your big story or not? Drew Webb is handing this thing to you on a silver platter, and he needs our help. Bec needs our help." Patric tightly grabs Tim by the forearm and squints his eyes looking directly into Tim's baby blues.

"Yeah, but..."

Patric cuts him off immediately and nearly cuts off the circulation in Tim's right arm. He feels the adrenaline running through his body as if the blood in his veins have been injected with it. He has no idea exactly how hard he is squeezing Tim's arm. He gently lets go, "We've got to get Becca out of there. I knew something was very wrong with this whole picture and with this so-called client, from the very beginning."

"Okay, sorry to keep you waiting." Susan flips around on her office chair and extends her hand. "Susan McCall, pleasure to make your acquaintance. Let's get your arrangements taken care of."

* * * * *

DOWN THE HALL A VERY ANXIOUS DREW WEBB is on the telephone. "Maggie, hello Drew Webb. I'm so glad I caught you in."

"Hello Judge Webb, how are you?" Maggie senses something is wrong by the urgency in his voice.

"A little unsettled at the moment. Do you happen to know where Rebecca might be?"

"Yes...she left this morning for the Bahamas for the weekend. Is there a problem? I'm a little surprised actually that she hadn't mentioned it to you. It did come rather suddenly, but I'm still a little shocked she hadn't told you." Maggie's voice obviously bewildered. Rebecca is so close to her father, it is really odd that she wouldn't have told him of her plans.

"Everything is just fine, Maggie. Just some family business I needed to discuss with her. You don't happen to know where she might be staying?"

"At the Ocean Club." Maggie responds as if he should know where she would be staying.

"Of course. Thanks Maggie. I've missed seeing you at the house this summer. Rebecca says you are doing well." Drew is calm and cordial, but hurried, talking quickly and wanting to gentlemanly finish this phone call.

"Thanks, yes. I'm sorry I haven't made it up this summer."

"Perhaps another time. I need to track down my daughter. Thanks again for your help, Maggie."

"Pleasure. She seemed excited to be going back to the Ocean Club. She was hoping to see some old friends..." Before Maggie could finish, he disconnected the call. "Must be something urgent," Maggie thought aloud as she went back about her day at Rebecca's apartment.

Webb immediately hits the intercom to Susan's desk. "Susan, are Tim and Patric still with you?"

"Yes, I am working on finalizing their flights now." Susan responds hastily in complete understanding of the urgency. She has worked for the Judge for many years and knows him like the back of her soft and manicured hands.

"Patric, she's at the Ocean Club. I will leave a message in her room and I am going to call a dear friend of mine who lives in Ocean Club Estates, Will Lightborne, and ask him to ride over to the club and look for her and take her back to his house. I need you guys to get down there and make sure she is alright. Can you leave right away? Time is of the essence." Webb is still talking very fast. The gravity of the situation is not misunderstood.

"Not a problem sir." Patric's voice comes over the intercom with confidence trying again to ease the mind of Rebecca's father.

"Thanks Patric, I am counting on you two. I will be in touch and will be there myself as soon as possible. Tim, I really appreciate your sacrifice right now. I know it's tough to leave an expectant mom for a day or two, but I will make it up to you both." Webb disconnects the intercom with his index finger and re-dials the phone quickly. This time to the Bahamas where he thankfully finds his old friend Will Lightborne at home. "Will, hello, it's Drew Webb." There is a pause. "Yes it has been a while, how is your family?" Another pause. "That's great. Will, I need your help. Rebecca is at the Ocean Club and I wondered if I could bother you to go over there and get her for me. Perhaps you could bring her back to your house and have her call me from there." Another pause. "Everything is fine. I am just having trouble reaching her and there is some rather urgent family business that I need to speak with her about. I would really appreciate it Will. It is a matter of some urgency. I will fill you in on the details later." One last pause. "I am in your debt."

125

SEVERAL FEET DOWN THE CORRIDOR OF Rooney, Stein, Rosen and Webb, Susan McCall works diligently to make arrangements. Her short red hair pushed behind her ears and her brown reading glasses pierce the end of her dainty ivory nose.

"I can't just leave right away." Tim still in panic mode.

"Oh yes you can. Webb will make it up to you." Patric snickers a bit somewhat making fun of his panic stricken friend.

"Great, just great. Wonder if he is going to call my pregnant, hormonal wife and tell her that I have to go to the Bahamas for a couple of days to save his daughter." Tim is not amused and is fairly certain Maureen isn't going to be either. She is a wonderful and understanding wife, but this one, might just be a bit beyond the ordinary call of a talented up-and-coming New York Times writer.

"Or, to get the biggest story of your career? Come on man, we need to get our shit together here. Mo will understand, trust me. Hormonal or not, she will get it. It's only going to be for a day or two. Maybe her mom would come stay with her until we get back." Pacifying his friend, Patric understands Tim's hesitation, especially now, but he needs his help and after all, this is for Tim's big story. The one he has been waiting for his entire career. It will catapult him to the next level at the Times, something the writer is very much ready for, both in timing and talent.

"Okay, here you go." Susan turns around from her printer and hands over airline documents. "Good luck. If you guys need anything, don't hesitate to call me. I will get you through to Judge Webb right away."

"Thanks Susan." Tim reaches out to grab the boarding passes and itineraries with an unhappy smirk on his face as if someone just handed him an expensive speeding ticket. Patric also thanks Susan and the two walk quickly down the hallway and out of the building.

"I don't believe this. I do not believe we are actually fucking doing this." Tim, still in shock, as if the world has taken over his every movement. His actions are completely out of his own control, like a puppet on a string.

"Come on Timbo. This is your big break. Think positive." With a big pat on the back Patric offers encouragement and appreciation.

"Bull shit. This is about saving the love of your life and you know it."

"She's your friend too, T and she'd be there for you buddy." If encouragement didn't make Tim feel good about what they were doing perhaps guilt will. "I need to go by my apartment and pick up some equipment and a few things. I'll come to your place and we'll have a cab pick us up there for the airport. Go home and tell Mo how much you love her and I'll see you in an hour or so." In total strategic mode, Patric begins planning their mission.

Tim, though hesitant, is responsive. "I know. You are absolutely right. I'll see you in an hour. So much for the cold one."

* * * * *

CHAPTER TWELVE

THE LONG WHITE STRETCH LIMOSUINE COMES to a gentle stop on Paradise Island Drive to make the left turn and pass the familiar pink stucco British Colonial welcome gate. *One and Only Ocean Club, Private, Members and Guests Only.* Lush tropical landscape lines both sides of the private entrance way, stately coconut and banana palms nearly cascade completely over the drive. Birds of Paradise seem to grow from the trunks of Royal Ponsiana and hibiscus blooms explode in every pastel imaginable. The beautiful property located on the northeast corner of what was once called Hog Island, was acquired by Axel Werner Glen, Swedish industrialist after he anchored his yacht on the north shore in 1939 and was totally taken by its incredible beauty. Inspired by the Chateau de Versailles in France, he nurtured the property with decadently landscaped gardens and built his private paradise estate. The re-knowned and eccentric Huntington Hartford, A & P Tea Company heir, purchased the island from the Swede in 1962 and built the original 50 room exclusive Ocean Club Resort, what is now the One & Only Ocean Club's Hartford Building. Hartford petitioned the Bahamian government to change the name of the island to Paradise, marking the beginning of the iconic legendary resort.

Huntington Hartford used the Ocean Club to entertain friends and kings, celebrities and royalty. William Randolph Hearst, Richard Nixon, and the Beatles were among his frequent guests. He improved upon the lush gardens Werner-Glen developed with marble statues, lily ponds and a 12th century cloister barged from France and reconstructed at the end of the terraced garden. Rebecca always felt a special connection here and hoped she would marry here, one day, at the Cloister in the garden with Nassau Harbor gleaming and the setting sun as witness. Though Hartford eventually sold the property and left the island, he returned to Nassau and spent his last years living at Lyford Cay Club with his youngest daughter Juliet.

Two Bond films highlighted the Ocean Club, Casino Royale and Thunderball in the late 1960's, beginning the great friendship between Hartford and Sean Connery, who still resides there today more than 40 years after he discovered the area's reverent beauty.

The guard nods the limo through and opens the lovely white wrought iron gate. Rebecca feels the skin on her arms tighten with goose bumps. Is it the excitement of being back to this wonderful place that she has missed so much, or the anxiety of meeting Geoffrey Zandieh here, in this familiar environment. The limo comes to a gentle stop at the elegantly understated British Colonial entrance. One of the Ocean Club staff greets the car and opens the car door. Rebecca steps out of the car and takes a long deep breath inhaling the balmy tropical air. The moist salt air fills her lungs and warms her body from the inside, she looks up into the deep blue sky and smiles. "I am home" a familiar voice from within her speaks.

"Miss Webb?" recognized and greeted by the Ocean Club staffer.

"Terrence, how are you? You as are handsome as ever." They embrace in a friendly hug.

"Doing fine, it has been a long time since you were here with us." Terrence directs the valet personnel to unload Rebecca's luggage from the trunk of the limousine and take it inside.

"Too long. It feels wonderful to be back here."

"How is Judge Webb?"

"He is fine Terrence, thanks for asking. I need to get him to come back as well. It's been very hard, but I think he is finally coming around." They walk under the covered polished stone entrance toward large glass double doors. Bright white pillars adorn the pink stucco building and cedar shake roof. Simple, tropical and elegant.

The doorman awaits and guides Rebecca into the marbled entry foyer leading into the ebony wood floored library. She turns back, "Thanks Terrence. Great to see you," and enters to the reception.

"Hello. Checking in, Webb, Rebecca Webb."

"Welcome back to the Ocean Club." The receptionist hands Rebecca an envelope and a key. "Your room is taken care of and I have taken the liberty of having your bags sent directly to your room. Is there anything else I can arrange for you at this time?"

"No, thank you." Rebecca opens the envelope. The card reads, "Very cold champagne waiting in the library." She smiles and walks around the corner to the library where Geoffrey Zandieh awaits at the bar. He stands, champagne in hand and walks toward her.

With a soft platonic kiss on the cheek, he hands her the glass, "Welcome to Paradise."

"Thanks," she laughs. "Welcome to you." The effervescence of the champagne tickles her nose as she takes the glass to her lips. They have a seat on the sofa next to the bar.

"Veuve Cliquot?" Geoffrey awaits her approval.

"But of course. It would be rude not to. How ever did you know?" Rebecca looks up at the bartender. "Hello Valentino."

"Nice to see you again Miss Webb, everyting is good?"

"Fine Tino, how about you?"

"Everyting good. Nice to have you back." spoken in true Bahamian.

Rebecca and Geoffrey toast glasses and both sip their champagne. What a way to end a very stressful week, she thinks to herself. The Ocean Club, blue sky, salt air and cold bubbles. Looking at the ocean she lets out a long sigh of relaxation.

"You seem to be quite the celebrity here. I was not aware that you were so well known at the Ocean Club." Geoffrey comments as he looks to her with piercing adoration. For the first time she feels it, she more than senses it, and it hits her right between the eyes. She immediately turns again to the ocean view to break eye contact. For a moment she feels light headed, almost faint. Her hands are clammy and cold and she feels the color leaving her face as if something were draining the energy straight from her soul. Taking another sip of champagne, and a very deep breath, she thinks, "it's okay, calm down, we're fine." Turning back toward Geoffrey, she slowly responds, "My family used to spend quite a lot of time here."

"So I gather. How was your trip?" Sensing she is uncomfortable , he tries to make simple conversation.

Rebecca complies. "Perfectly uneventful, how was London?"

"Perfectly dreary, as usual." They both chuckle a bit as Rebecca begins to feel more comfortable with him. Behold the power of bubbles when you need them.

"I brought the final proposal for your portfolio. I hope it meets with your approval." She reaches in her bag and hands Geoffrey an envelope.

"Thank you. You certainly get right to business don't you Miss Webb. How is your champagne?"

"Wonderful, thanks. And you certainly get right to changing the subject, don't you Mr. Zandieh?" She squints her eyes, dipping her head forward, chin to her chest with a playful glare in his direction. "Have you finished your other business here?" Perhaps it was just the travel, lack of sleep the night before or finally exhaling after a busy and stressful week...month, but the bubbles seem to be going straight to her head.

"Almost." Geoffrey responds quickly.

Once again, she can't help turning toward the view, the blue water a magnet to her beautiful eyes. "You know as many times as I have seen this view, it is even more amazing than I remember. The water is just mesmerizing, isn't it? The color is so incredible."

"So now I know a little more about you, your favorite color anyway."

"Yes," she smiles. "This is so lovely, but I really need to get settled in to my room, make a few calls, freshen up a bit. Would you excuse me?"

"Of course. Could we meet back here for dinner? 7:00 ish?" He gets up and reaches for her hand to help her out of the chair in such gentlemanly fashion. Rebecca takes his hand and also stands.

"That would be great. Thanks for the champagne. I'm feeling a little tired, I may even catch a quick power nap before dinner." She starts toward the door and he pulls her back to kiss her gently on the cheek. She is taken back by this kiss and pulls away. Yes, of course he has kissed her in a friendly way before, but this time is different, this time perhaps forceful, but in a gentle way, a dangerous way. Letting go of her hand, Geoffrey takes a step back as she turns and walks toward the guest rooms. He continues to watch her walk, her every move, until she strolls out of his sight.

Rebecca arrives at her suite and walks directly to open the sliding glass door on the ocean. Taking another deep breath of the balmy salt air, she leaves the door open to feel the ocean breeze and lies down on the bed. The sound of the surf dancing against the sand relaxes her as she lies there thinking about Geoffrey Zandieh, this attractive man whom she is here with. Closing her eyes, she listens to the music of the gentle surf and pictures him as he greeted her this afternoon in his soft light blue suit, crisp open white linen shirt against his dark skin. His dark hair perfectly coiffed, symmetrical face and dark eyes, so focused on her. The red message light is flashing, but she falls deeply asleep before she even has a chance to notice.

The phone is ringing, but she does not wake up. The sheer draperies flow in the ocean breeze into the room and out through the open door as if to mimick the very surf itself. Through the open door lurks Geoffrey Zandieh, somehow knowing that Rebecca would be at this time in deep, unconscious sleep. He goes to her bed and sits gently beside her swiping the back of his hand over her soft cheek then running his manicured fingers through her lovely hair. The orange glow of the sunset lays across her weak mouth, distinctly high cheek bones and her peaceful eyes as she lay sleeping. He looks at her and thinks, "I have wanted you since the first time I saw you, and have thought of little else since that moment." Sitting very still by her side, he says to her what he had never allowed himself to say.

"Since the first time I saw you...everything, even the way your eyes would try to avoid mine, made me want you. It was as if at our every meeting you thought so safe, you wanted to trust me, and for me to think of you as you deserve. Obviously you did hence you would not be here now, but don't you know how much I have betrayed you? A true dichotomy, the most inspiring encounter of my life, and perhaps the only person I have truly respected, even trusted...how could I be doing this to you? Do you not know who I am? A primal desire should be unthinkable. That deprecating need which should never touch you, though I have never wanted anyone but you and never anything more...why did it have to be under these circumstances?"

"I had not known what it was to truly want it until I saw you for the very first time. I thought I could not be broken by it, by you. Would you want to know what I think when I look at you, when I lie awake at night and wish for all of this to be behind us, that we could have met somehow, somewhere, but not here. When I hear your voice on the phone, and could not drive this feeling away. To do to you what you do not understand and to know that it is I who has done this to you. And now, to think of you in animalistic terms, but it is desire from my heart, the very core of my soul and not of humanistic need."

He stops and watches the sun begin to descend towards the calm sea marking the end of this dreadful day. He turns back to her and again brushes the side of her face with his hand. Continuing to speak softly to her, he goes on. "My sweet dear Rebecca. Don't you know that I have never experienced a feeling like this before? To wish that you would also want me on these terms and to see your wonderful soul also need me, to watch you take on the world with your innocence and strength, then to see you, with me, submitting to my physical whims and desires. I am in love with you, and both truly blessed and cursed for it. I only hope, though it is not realistic to believe, that when this is over, you could forgive this man who loves you so very much."

The phone rings again and Geoffrey, though startled at first, snaps back to reality, clearing his mind and realizing it is time to get on with this business. "How long have I been sitting here?" he asks himself. "If only for a moment, it is a moment I will treasure always."

It is almost dark now and the sun has well made its final plunge into the seemingly black ocean. All that is left are the dark shadows of palms swaying in the breeze against the deep purple water colored sky. This day is done.

* * * * *

REBECCA WAKES, SOMEWHERE, STILL DROWSY but not in her beautiful Ocean Club Suite. She looks around and though her mind is still a bit fuzzy, she knows this is not where she is supposed to be. Being on enough large yachts to know, she finds herself in a stateroom, her LV handbag on the chair beside the berth. "What a hangover," she thinks to herself rubbing her temples. Trying to get herself together, she looks around this rich and lavish room. Hues of deep burgundy and gold, cherry wood cabinets and mirrored ceiling. All of a sudden, she gets a very bad feeling as the door opens and Geoffrey Zandieh joins her in the stateroom.

"Am I dreaming? What happened? I couldn't have gotten that hammered from one glass of champagne. Where are we?"

"I'm sorry, how are you feeling?" Geoffrey is caring and gentle in his response, but still this is making no sense to Rebecca whatsoever.

"A bit confused at the moment, and with a hell of a hangover. Geoffrey what's going on?"

"I thought a little cruise might be fun." He makes light of the situation and Rebecca obviously realizes there is much more to this than a cruise.

"Did you think to ask me first?" she asks with a most serious and unamused tone.

"I had to be certain your answer would be yes. I'm sorry Rebecca. Do you remember that little piece of business that I needed to take care of here?"

"It's me? Why? I really don't understand what is going on here Geoffrey. Does this have something to do with my father?" All of a sudden it comes together like the final pieces of a jigsaw puzzle. She still doesn't know exactly why she is here, but after years of her family trying to avoid just such a situation while her father was with the court system, FBI and CIA, she knew it probably wasn't good.

"Rebecca, the situation is this and I want to be as honest with you as possible. There are members of your government, very powerful members, who believe your father is putting his nose into something that isn't really any of his business and you are now their insurance policy that he will not pursue this business any further."

"Knowing my father, he already has the FBI looking for me."

"Perhaps that is so, but by the time they find you, it won't matter any longer."

"What are you saying Geoffrey? Do you plan to kill me? If it is something that important, I don't think my father would ever stop pursuing this so-called business."

"My intentions are not to harm you in any way, please believe that. These people just need a little time to make sure your father doesn't interfere with their plans for some very influential people. After that, you are on your own, free to go. Rebecca, please believe me when I say that it IS a matter of international importance."

"And you disappear into thin air?" Her fear turns to anger.

"Something like that. You won't be harmed Rebecca, I will see to that. Please just enjoy some time on these beautiful waters. I hate to leave a great vacation, with a truly incredible woman, but I must be heading back to Europe. It was a pleasure spending time with you. Perhaps in a different world or even a different time..." he stops, though he wants to continue. He wants very much to tell her how he feels about her, and even more, would like to take her back to Europe with him, but he knows this is impossible now. They would both be in grave danger and more than anything now, he just wants to be able to protect her. He is in too deep, not to finish the job, but to accomplish this and keep her out of harms way, is all there is now.

"C'est la vie, then." She says in a very angry tone and turns her head away from Geoffrey, she does not even want to look at him.

"Please try to understand, Rebecca. Enjoy yourself. It is the best thing that you can do. I have arranged for every luxury here for you, anything you desire. I will send for you when this is all over and you will be free to do whatever you need to do at that time. In the meantime, Captain Rolle, will see to it that you are comfortable and well cared for. Again, I am sorry." Still she will not look at him, and out of deep respect for her, he does not approach. "Au revoir Miss Rebecca Webb. Until we meet again..."

Geoffrey leaves the stateroom and Captain Rolle pops his head in to greet his new guest. "Hello Miss Webb. Welcome to the Renaissance. I understand that you will be cruising with us for a little while. Please let me know if there is anything that myself or my crew can do for you. I think you'll find everything you need aboard. Mr. Zandieh has arranged for many of your favorite comforts. You will find all of your things in the closet here in the stateroom. Please make yourself at home. Welcome aboard madam."

Rebecca turns to the Captain, "Captain, there is something you could do for me. When Mr. Zandieh departs the Renaissance, could you please take me back to Nassau?" She pleads, knowing full well what answer lies ahead.

"I am so sorry Miss Webb. I am afraid that is not possible at the moment, but in due time. When I get the call from Mr. Zandieh, you will be returned straight away. You have my word on that. If that is all for now, I will leave you alone. Please use the intercom if you need anything and try to relax and enjoy your time on board with us. When you are ready to join us on deck, we will be honored to have you." Captain Rolle is sympathetic, yet he knows he also has a job to do, and is committed to carrying out his orders as well.

The Captain leaves the stateroom and closes the door behind him. Rebecca gets up and looks out the stateroom window. All she can see is blue water for miles and two gentlemen on a small boat departing.

One of the men is Geoffrey Zandieh. She moves shakily to the bathroom door, obviously still a bit dizzy from the drugs in her champagne. Looking in the mirror, she thinks that all she wants at this moment is her toothbrush. Of course, without a detail missing, her cosmetic bag is awaiting on the marble vanity. Rebecca laughs for a moment as she opens the bag to get her toothbrush, and then begins to cry, sinking to the floor like a wet dishrag. It is as if something has sucked every bit of life from her body. There she sits, head resting against the cold cabinet door, tears streaming down her cheeks, face in her hands, sobbing uncontrollably.

"How the hell could I have been so ridiculously stupid," she cries out then gathers herself together and goes to her handbag left on the chair next to the berth. Fumbling through the bag, still a bit shaken and half-drunk still from the night-nighty cocktail, she finds her cell phone.

"Oh my God. Why wouldn't he take my phone?" She turns it on impatiently awaiting for it to boot. "Come on, come on…" The apple lights up the screen, but she notices the signal is weak, quite weak. In addition, the battery is not much better. The signal fails. "Come on, give me a signal…something," but nothing. She is well outside of cell phone range and apparently no WIFI is available on the boat, at least not at this juncture. Rebecca goes back to the vanity and retrieves the toothbrush from her bag. She begins brushing her teeth so hard she may permanently destroy the enamel. She is coming back to life now and the adrenaline is kicking in…so much in fact her gums begin to bleed, though she does not notice until rinsing, watching the blood washing down the drain in the sink. Determined and just plain pissed off at this point, she takes a hair tie from her cosmetic case and pulls her beautiful locks back into a ponytail high on her head. Still in the same clothing she wore on arrival in Nassau, she splashes cold water on her face and pats dry with a soft white towel with *Renaissance* boldly embroidered in gold stitching.

Filtered rays of the sun glare through the stateroom window making floating dust particles visible through the gleaming light. Rebecca finds her sunglasses and very deliberately leaves the stateroom, up the steps to the main deck. There are 4 crewmen dressed in starched whites with gold tasseled epaulets, seemingly very professional. Her sunglasses hiding her puffy, dark circled and blood shot eyes, she is greeted politely by every one of them with an acknowledging nod, but no words are spoken. "I wonder what they have been told about me?" She thinks to herself. "They probably think I am just another one of Geoffrey Zandieh's women here for a little fun in the sun. How could I have been to stupid." She speaks under her breath. Captain Rolle comes from the bridge.

"Miss Webb, how lovely to see you on deck. Aren't these waters the most beautiful you have ever seen?" The Captain tries to make her feel comfortable, though he senses her tense anxiety. Rebecca feels a tear coming down her cheek quickly being blown dry by the strong trade winds, at least 30 knots, though the surf is relatively calm, 3-4 foot seas maximum and on the 80 foot Renaissance, hardly a bump.

"Yes, it is beautiful," she responds as she looks around trying to get some idea as to where in the world they are. She knew these waters fairly well as a young girl. Surely there was going to be something recognizable, but still only deep turquoise waters were in sight for as far as the eye could see. Trying to get re-orientated, Rebecca notices the time on her watch, 8:00, but is it am or pm? The sun seems to be starting to set in the distance, or is it only continuing to rise as it ascends into a new day? Is this Saturday? Sunday? Just how long have I been asleep? Overwhelmed by her frustration, the tears begin to flow and Captain Rolle is acutely aware of her fear.

"What can we get for you Miss Webb?" again the Captain politely tries to help Rebecca feel comfortable, with his gentle and kind manner. She would like to appreciate his efforts, but in light of the circumstances, finds it repulsively redundant. She turns away.

CHAPTER THIRTEEN

WITH A GENTLE SCREACH, THE WHEELS OF THE 737 hit the ground. "Ladies and gentlemen, Welcome to Nassau. We should be at the gate momentarily." The flight attendant announces the arrival of Delta flight 373 from Laguardia.

Arousing from his sleep, Tim turns to his seat mate and friend, "If I live through this, my wife is going to kill me."

"She won't kill you partner, she doesn't want to be a single mom." Patric jests as he slaps his friend sharply on the thigh.

"Very funny asshole." Tim doesn't think it is so funny.

"Lighten up my friend. Let's get our business done here and get your paranoid ass back to the city."

"Any ideas on how we are going to find a needle in a haystack?" Tim is already doubting the mission. "A very fine needle, I might add but what the fuck?"

"I just wish we could have gotten here last night. We've already lost a day. Webb's friend said that she has definitely been out of site since late yesterday. I know some guys at the marina that usually know everything going down on PI. It's a start." Patric seems confident and courageously determined.

Tim and Patric deboard the plane, get through customs, have their passports stamped and then walk outside to get a cab. "Hurricane Hole, please." Patric forcefully asks the driver.

"Marina buddy?"

"Yes, please. We are in a hurry if you don't mind...thanks." Patric is more than in a hurry, he is just damn impatient and ready to get this show on the road. So much so he is oblivious to the surroundings, and even his partner on this mission.

Sweat begins to form droplets on Patric's temples and run fluidly down the sides of his face. A hot balmy day in Nassau, and of course, the cab has no air conditioning, though the balmy breeze coming through the windows offers some relief. Patric's heart begins to beat fast and hard with anxiety. This car just can't go fast enough and the clock is ticking, all too quickly. Whatever Zandieh's plans are for Rebecca, both gentlemen know, are not in her best interest and time is of the essence in locating their friend and finding a way to get her home. The bridge to Paradise Island is finally visible in the distance.

"If we can just get through town without much traffic on Bay Street we're golden." Patric says looking out the window to the left with the bridge in sight. "I left a message for one of the captains who looks after Mer Soleil to meet us at the boat. I asked him to dig around for any scoop at the marina. Hopefully he'll have something for us."

"You are really starting to act like an investigative reporter, it's a little scary dude. What happened to the aloof, artsy photographer I used to know?" Tim tries to make light conversation as they continue through Nassau. "You have always been a curious sucker, though."

"Especially when it comes to something I have a great deal of interest in. I'm worried about her T, I'm really worried." The two men have a moment of piercing eye contact and Patric turns again to look out the window. Fortunately, the usual slow moving and heavy traffic is not so bad today as they make their way through downtown to the bridge.

Patric can see the marina on the other side as well as the mast of Mer Soleil as it sways about in the swirling trade winds. White caps are forming in the harbor and the waves are bouncing into and off of the pier. Hoping Girard got his message, he pulls out his phone to call.

"Hey man, you get my message?" (pause) "We're on the bridge."

Patric puts the phone back in his pocket and turns to Tim. "Girard's at the boat. If anything odd is happening on PI, he'll have the inside."

A VERY SOLEMN DREW WEBB IS VERY QUICKLY putting together a few things in his large tailored mahogany closet at Morgan Manor and packing a small bag to leave the country. Vibrating in his pocket, Drew takes his cell phone and, looking at the number calling in, he answers.

"Bill, good afternoon. Thanks for sparing Tim Connelly for a day or two."

"My pleasure Drew. What's going on?" There is dignified concern in Bill Weller's voice on the other end of the phone.

"They have Rebecca, Bill. I never dreamed these idiots would use my daughter. How foolish."

"Your theories are obviously close, if not right on. What about Rebecca, what can I do to help?" Weller responds.

"I have already spoken with some old friends at the FBI and they are on it. We will get her home safely. I am hoping Tim and Patric can come up with some good information on the ground in Nassau and by the time I arrive with proper authorities they might have some idea of where my guys can find her. I just can't believe I let it get out of control where Rebecca is concerned. We need to proceed quietly however, very quietly. I'll keep you posted."

"Let me know what I can do. Tim is an excellent investigative journalist. If there is any information to be found on the ground there, he and Taylor will be able to find it." Weller is supportive and confident.

"Thanks Bill, I'll be in touch." Putting the phone back into his pocket, Drew closes his travel bag and leaves the room. The Honorable Drew Webb and former FBI director is in full mission mode and on his way to the Bahamas to recover his most meaningful case...his daughter.

* * * * *

THE WIND GUSTS AS TIM AND PATRIC MAKE THEIR WAY down the dock to the Mer Soleil. Waiting for them at the boat is Girard. "Hello my friend."

"Hi, Girard." The two shake hands. "This is a good friend and business associate of mine, Tim Connelly." Girard reaches to shake Tim's hand also.

"What do you hear, Girard? Anything unusual on PI the last 48 hours or so?" Patric cuts right to the chase and throws his bag onto the deck of Mer Soleil.

"Nothing more than the usual stolen dinghy's and drug runners. Anything in particular you are looking for?"

"I'm looking for a friend of mine actually."

Girard interjects, "Blonde or brunette?" chuckling.

"Very funny Girard." Patric pauses. "She is blonde actually..."

Girard interrupts again, "A man after my own desires."

Becoming a little abrupt and not appreciating the interruptions, Patric cuts back in, "Anyway, she was supposed to be at Ocean Club this weekend and apparently decided not to stay there. Have you seen an attractive blonde on any of the yachts here this weekend?"

"About a hundred of them." Girard laughs again. "What's so special about this one?"

"Long story Girard, but I think my friend may be in trouble man."

"Drugs?" Girard asks.

"No, nothing like that. But she may be with someone that she is trying to get away from, someone who has her here against her will."

Tim now gets involved in the conversation. "Girard, could you ask around and see if anyone may have noticed a woman seemingly uncomfortable, or with someone in an awkward situation."

"So, the lady is with someone, I am assuming another man?" Girard implies. "A nasty love triangle?"

"Girard, this is really important and is not of a personal nature, but the lady is in danger and we really need to find her. Can you dig around, on the QT?" Making it clear that this is business and not "monkey business" Tim changes Girard's tone from gossipy dock hand to professional boat captain.

"This is serious?" Girard looks at his friend Patric Taylor.

"Yeah, man, real serious. Can you see what you can find out?"

"I'll check with some of the guys here at the marina and over at the Atlantis marina also to see if they remember anything like this. Will you be hanging here on the boat?"

"Either here or on my cell. Let me know if you hear anything. I don't know where else to start. I told my friend Tim here that if anything was going down on PI, you were the man that could find out." Seemingly a bit desperate and obviously without any other ideas, Patric thanks Girard and he and Tim climb aboard the Mer Soleil.

"What do you think Tim, should we head down to the Ocean Club and nose around there? We know someone there had to see her before she disappeared. You're the investigator, what do you think?"

"Good idea Padre. Let's do it. It's the only lead we have to go on at the moment. We'll find her." Trying to reassure his friend Tim gives Patric a friendly pat on the back.

Patric opens the hatch and throws their bags below, slamming the hatch door closed. Reaching in the aft deck cooler, he throws Tim a cold bottle of water, then grabbing one for himself. "Let's go."

* * * * *

WALKING AROUND THE POLISHED TEAK DECK of the Renaissance, Rebecca hardly notices the strong winds or rough seas on this beautiful clear sunny day. Trying to think of a way out of this mess she realizes that other than Maggie, she told no one of her plans to go to the Bahamas...not even her father. Walking back inside through the galley, Rebecca notices some of her favorite wines, snacks, etc. Even in this captive and most uncomfortable moment, she can't help but to somehow muster a small smile amidst her bewilderment. "This is so bizarre," she thought. Her senses are finally beginning to return as she remembers that for whatever reason, her cell phone is still below. Quietly returning to the state room, locking the door behind her, "let's try this again," she whispers.

There is still very little signal. Feeling extremely weak, she slides down to the floor on the other side of the berth and away from the door. Hunched over and as quietly as possibly, she dials, somehow, automatically and unconsciously, her fingers gently touching Patric's cell phone number, one number at a time. Before she can say anything, Patric speaks loudly into the phone.

"Becca, where the hell are you?"

In a very low voice, just above a whisper, "Oh, Patric, I'm sorry, I don't know why my fingers just automatically..."

"Not important, tell me where you are." He cuts off her apology.

The phone begins to break up, "I have no signal, I hope you can hear me. I am on a yacht in the Bahamas called Renaissance. It's a Lazarra, probably 80ish. They took me from PI. Can you hear me?"

"You're breaking up Bec, are you okay? Tell me more about the boat."

"Renaissance." loudly, only hoping that he can hear her. The signal is gone. "Oh my God, Patric," she weeps. The phone falls to the floor.

145

Rebecca looks at the phone on the floor, it is dead, no signal left, no battery charge. Hugging her knees to her chest and placing her nose just between them, she begins to cry. There is a knock at the state room door.

"Miss Webb. Unlock the door please. I know that you must be upset, but please unlock the door. Mr. Z made it clear that we are to take good care of you and make sure that you are comfortable. Please try to find a way to enjoy yourself. Everything will be fine. It should only be a few days before I am able to return you to Nassau."

Rebecca opens the door. "What's all this about Captain Rolle? Please tell me what this is about."

"Honestly, madam, I really have no idea, but our orders are clear."

"Orders from whom? From Geoffrey? Who is giving the orders?"

"Please don't make trouble. My orders are from Mr. Zandieh, and he is smart enough not to tell me anything more. He only told me that you are precious cargo and to be well cared for. His orders are from some very influential people but I do not know who. Mr. Z cares for you. He will make sure that nothing happens to you." Captain Rolle tries to calm Rebecca, her head resting against the opened door, tears streaming down her lovely face.

"He obviously cares more for these influential people of his than he does for me. My father is very influential also. I know he is not going to just let me be missing for a few days and not do anything about it." She is stern in her response to the good Captain as she thinks to herself. "Get a grip Rebecca, he doesn't even know your away."

Captain Rolle, steps back. "The chef has prepared you a lovely lunch on deck. I think it will help you feel better. I will leave you alone." He turns to walk up the stairs to the salon.

"Okay. Give me a moment to get myself together." She wipes her tears away.

"As you wish." The Captain responds as he makes his way up the steps. "See you on deck." Rebecca goes back to retrieve her phone from the floor and tries one more time to turn it back on. No success, it is totally dead now. She hurls it across the stateroom and rummages through her bag to find something comfortable to wear. Looking out the port hole she thinks of Patric. "God I hope that Patric was able to hear me. If he just got the name of the boat, he could surely track me down...right?" she whispers again to herself. "What am I thinking? Patric doesn't know I'm missing either. He probably thinks I'm crazy."

She finds an exercise halter and pair of yoga pants in her bag and puts them on. She washes her face and applies sunscreen to her cheeks, nose and forehead rubbing in gently, avoiding her very red, bloodshot eyes. "I look horrible," she thinks to herself looking in the mirror as a pair of dark puffy eyes stare back at her.

Taking a deep breath, Rebecca gathers her thoughts and pulls herself together. She walks through the dark walled but sunlit stateroom as the light gleams in from the portholes and forms a sunny spot on the edge of the berth. She sits down for a moment, feeling much better as the sun's rays soothe her tenseness. Stretching her neck, she can feel each muscle beginning to unfold, to release, and yet, she feels stronger now, more deliberate in thought. Thinking quietly she picks up the phone from the floor and holds it to her chest. "Funny isn't it that in the midst of crisis, who is it that I should call. Who is it that I turn to, reach out for, without even a conscious thought. Without hesitation and with unintentional clarity. It is the one who I share more than a past, more than friendship or even a foolish schoolgirl crush. He is part of me, part of my very soul, my other half. The one who completes my thoughts, my purpose, my life. Did it take a situation as grave as this, to bring me to my senses, to bring me this clarity of who I am, and with whom I am meant to share my life. Perhaps, now I can finally accept it, though perhaps now, it is too late.

BACK AT HURRICANE HOLE MARINA, PATRIC tries desperately to call Rebecca back, but the phone now goes directly into voice mail.

"Was that Becca?" Tim is in shock.

"Damnit. I can't get her back. The connection was terrible, I barely could make out anything she was saying. I think she is on a boat, a yacht, somewhere out there."

"How the hell was she able to call?" Tim still in shock.

"I have no idea, but the call was from her cell phone. I don't think I'll be able to re-connect. The signal was too weak."

"What did she say?"

"She tried to tell me the name of the boat, but I couldn't make it out. Something like...shit...I don't know. The connection was so bad. Damnit!" Patric shows intense frustration.

"Think my man. What did it sound like?" Tim is encouraging.

"Fuck, I don't know. R word, I think." He dials Girard. "Girard, I need ya buddy. You still here at the marina?"

"T, at least we know she is definitely on a yacht, somewhere in the Bahamas, since sometime late yesterday, so she can't be that far from here. And, she is okay, at least so far. She didn't mention landmarks, I am guessing wherever she is right now at least, all she can see is blue water. Let's charter a sea plane and take a look around from the air." Patric begins to think of a plan, a way to find her.

"She could be anywhere out there. How the hell are we going to know what frickin' direction to go?"

"I don't know man, but we need to get out there. Let's talk to some of the dock hands here, they usually have a pretty good idea about large boats coming in and out of PI." Patric looks up as Girard approaches.

148

"What's up?" Girard walking quickly along the dock back to Mer Soleil. "You find your friend?"

"Girard, do know of a Lazarra, 80ish that may be hailing from PI?"

"Several of them, you don't know the name?"

"No. If I heard it I might be able to recall it." Patric is not sure.

"This is where you think your lady friend may be?"

"Yes Girard. Have you noticed any sort of strange 70-80 footers come in and out recently?"

Girard yells out to one of the dock hands close by. "Hey Trevor, what 80 footers have gone out of the harbor in the past couple of days? Any ideas?"

The dock hand responds, "I've only seen a couple come through Nassau Harbor this week. Mostly charters. Who you lookin' for?"

"My friend is looking for a pretty blonde." Girard tries to add a little levity to the situation.

"Yeah. Me too. What does this one look like?" The dock hand smiles, puts down what he is working on and approaches the boat.

"We think she was taken aboard against her will, probably sometime during the night. Anything like that sound familiar to you?" The diligent reporter Tim Connelly persists.

"Last night?" asks the dock hand.

"We don't know for sure, but most likely it was last night. Wouldn't you say partner?" Tim looks toward Patric who nods affirmative.

"There was a yacht to go out in the middle of the night last night. Girard, what was that boat name?" Trevor is thinking. "Remember, it was the charter for that dark Ex-Pat. What was is called?"

149

"There was a Lazarra for charter that just came in here couple days ago." Girard is beginning to remember the boat. "Not a local crew, I didn't know any of the guys. Didn't see the Captain or notice any charter guests on the vessel, just the crew. It was gone when I got here early this morning."

"Girard, that English guy was on board. He was staying on board." Trevor recalls.

"Hold on." Girard takes his phone in hand and rings the marina office as he walks away from the boat to talk.

"I have a good idea that is where she is, Tim. I feel it. We need to find that boat." Patric's excitement restarts his internal engines, the adrenaline begins to pump. He feels confident that they are moving in the right direction.

Girard returns to the boat. "It was called Renaissance. The girls in the office think it was heading to the Exumas. They said the boat never officially checked-out of the marina but did call harbor control last night around ten pm."

"That's it Tim, that's what she was trying to say, I am sure of it. Thanks guys. Girard, do you know anyone we could charter a sea plane from? I want to get to Exumas." Patric presses on.

"Try Executive Air Support, they may have something. I'm not in the airplane business. I pretty much stick with things that float. I hope you find your lady. I'll be around if I can help or do anything here."

"Thanks Girard. You've been a great help already." Reaching in his pocket, Patric pulls out a $100 bill and hands it to Girard. "Take care of Trevor too, okay Girard?"

"Thank you sir." Trevor shakes Patric's hand. "I better get back to work. I'm around the Hole too, if you need a hand."

"Let's go T, we've got a plane to catch." Patric is anxious to get on the trail. They walk quickly toward the marina office where they will catch a cab to the charter FBO to find an available seaplane. At least they have a boat name and a possible, even probable, direction. Things seem to be falling into place and happening quickly as Patric is anxious to press on without even considering the possible danger ahead.

"Don't those sea planes have only one engine?" Thinking aloud, Tim really didn't want Patric to hear his concern, but hear it he did.

"Don't get the willies on me TC. We are in this together right?"

"Why don't you go check it out and I'll hang here at the boat . I could continue to the Ocean Club and gather as much information as I can over there." The expectant father is not crazy about the idea of getting on a single engine plane in gale force winds but he knows he really has no choice.

"Forget about it...you are coming with me," insists Patric.

"Yeah, yeah, I know."

"T, don't crap out on me now. Let's get to the airport."

"I'm with ya brother, you know that. Just thinking of my wife and kid. Sorry. Think we should give Webb a call on the way to the airport? I wonder why Bec didn't call him?"

"She probably did. I'm guessing that is why she called me. He knew we were already here. He probably told her to track us down so that we could get to her." Justifying the call, Patric hadn't had time to think about why she would attempt to reach him, but he was thrilled that she did and thrilled now to be on her trail. The cab ride to the airport will be a long one and he will think of nothing except finding his distressed Rebecca and bringing her back to safe harbor...bringing her home.

SEATED ALONE ABOARD A PRIVATE AIRCRAFT WAITING for take-off, Geoffrey Zandieh holds Rebecca's business card in his hand. Thinking of her he begins fondling the card through his fingers twirling it around each one. His cell phone rings. "Yes." He answers.

A very distinctive man's voice inquires, "What's the status of our project?"

Somewhat taken aback, Zandieh responds, "I wasn't expecting to hear from you directly."

The voice interrupts. "It has become apparent that your so called heat isn't working. Our problem here is getting worse. Can you turn the heat up? We don't want to know any details, and of course if anything were to go wrong..."

"I understand, of course, that goes with the territory. Your guest in Cuba is comfortable, but beginning to become antsy. What are your plans for him and when?"

"This is not your concern. Our plans for him haven't as yet been finalized, but it is imperative that you keep him content until closer to the election. More importantly right now, we have got to get these damn New York vigilantes under wraps. I don't care what you have to do. You have been paid very well to take care of this. Do what you must but the message needs to be stronger in order for these people to back off." This directive comes from the top, the controller of the mission who is obviously running thin on patience. Mr. Zandieh's patience is also depleting and it is obvious from where, actually who, this communication originated, that things are deteriorating on the other end. Drew Webb must have actually turned the heat up after the disappearance of his daughter, rather than backing off. "I like this man," Zandieh thinks to himself. Like his daughter, Geoffrey Zandieh also finds Drew Webb's resolve impressive. He smiles, still looking at the business card.

"You're not paying me that much you arrogant son of a bitch." Zandieh says aloud.

The pilot turns around to Mr. Zandieh, "We'll be underway in just a few minutes, Sir."

"There's been a change of plans." Zandieh informs the pilot.

* * * * *

CHAPTER FOURTEEN

THE RECEPTIONIST AT EXECUTIVE FLIGHT SERVICE is busy on the telephone while Patric and Tim try to patiently wait for assistance. She is an attractive Bahamian woman and based on the conversation the guys just eavesdropped on, very knowledgeable. Finally, she looks up to greet the impatient visitors. "May I help?"

"We'd like to charter a seaplane and pilot for this afternoon," very quickly Tim replies.

"Sir, I'm so sorry. We aren't chartering any longer this afternoon. It is nearly evening and with the winds picking up even more late this afternoon, it is just too dangerous now. Where do you need to go?"

"Heading toward Exumas, but we really need it this afternoon." Putting on his best pleading puppy dog eyes, Patric is hoping to at least get her to follow up further.

"I am very sorry sir."

"Forgive me for being rude Miss Laramore, is that Theresa Laramore?" He looks at her name tag and she smiles and nods. "May I possibly speak to your supervisor. It is a matter of some urgency"

Miss Laramore does feel that he is being rude and though rolling her dark eyes at them, she picks up the phone to call on her supervisor.

"Dude, if the lady says it isn't safe, maybe we should try something else." Tim, already not excited about the flight, is really losing interest now.

"Bec has to be horrified by now, we are not leaving her out there. It could be tomorrow before the conditions improve. She may not have a tomorrow, Tim, we have to get out there today." Patric is insistent. He is not taking no for an answer and will continue until he finds a pilot who is willing to fly even in these winds.

* * * * *

BACK ON BOARD THE RENAISSANCE, Rebecca goes on deck and sits down at the table for a bite of lunch. She is not the least bit hungry, but she is weak and knows she needs strength. It is a beautiful day on the water, the afternoon sun glistens on the foamy wake left behind by Renaissance as she travels south. Still only water in every direction, Rebecca stares into the distance, still hoping that Patric was able to make out just enough of what she said to be able to do something. Even if he did think she has lost her mind, he must know that for her to call him, something is awry. Surely, if nothing else, he would call my father, her mind is now moving in a thousand directions and a thousand miles per hour.

"Could I offer you a drink, cocktail...champagne perhaps?" The chef approaches his lone guest.

"No thanks. Last time I had champagne, I woke up..." She pauses. "I'm sorry, not important. Anyway, thank you, but just water would be fine."

"Very well then. We'll have lunch out for you very shortly." The chef returns to the galley.

Rebecca nibbles on the beautiful fruit bowl left on the table. The grapes are large, ripe and sweet. Maybe I am hungry, she thinks to herself as the introduction of just one grape to her system sends her stomach into the growl of a lion. She takes another and chews very slowly extracting all of the juice from the grape before finally swallowing its skin.

Looking into the sky, she spots a seaplane in the distance heading in the general direction of the Renaissance. "Could that be someone coming for me?" She continues to watch the plane's direction and stands in anticipation.

The plane continues to come closer and Rebecca notices the crew preparing lines on the stern swim platform. One of the mates places a beautiful lobster salad on the table for her, though her attention is focused only on the approaching plane. It lands in the water, and taxi's toward the boat. One of the crew men tosses a line to the pilot and pulls the plane into the platform. Geoffrey Zandieh steps down from the plane and makes his way up onto the aft deck. Though she is still taken by his suave appearance, she reminds herself that this is the jerk that drugged her, put her on a boat, and means harm of some form to her father. She sits back down at the table.

"Hello my dear Rebecca. You are looking lovely as usual. I trust the crew has taken good care of you." He approaches her but stops short of the table. "I see that they have provided you with a nice lunch."

"I'd ask you to join me, but…" She glares at him. "Geoffrey, what the hell is going on? Why are you doing this to me? To my father? I would like to have some understanding, please Geoffrey, please help me to understand what this is all about." She pleads with him, but with a strong tone. The drugs have worn off completely now, and her resolve has returned. No more intoxicated weepy tears.

"Rebecca, trust me…please."

"Trust you? Are you kidding me?" She turns away.

"Rebecca, please hear me out." He takes the seat next to her and rests his hand on the arm of her chair. She looks at him as he sits down next to her, then turns her head immediately in the opposite direction to avoid having eye contact. "Rebecca, I can't tell you what this is all about, but perhaps your father can when you get back to New York."

"And just when will that be?"

"The price of this job has gotten too high. Things have changed. I have changed. I only wish I could have changed before the situation had gone this far. You and I would have made a good team Rebecca."

She turns back to face her captor as he continues. "You see, I am really quite fond of you my dear and therefore you are of no use to me anymore, not as far as this mission is concerned."

"So...what...you are going to just dispose of me?"

"No, my darling girl, I am letting you go. I've instructed Captain Rolle to return you to Nassau. Your friends are there looking for you. You won't have any problems from me. I so wish things could be different for you and me Rebecca." He leans over to kiss her and again she turns away. Geoffrey stands and kisses her lightly on the top of her head. "Goodbye Rebecca Webb. It has been a pleasure. If we only had met in a different time, different place..."

He turns and walks gracefully back to the seaplane, then turns around one last time. The two engage in a moment of captive eye contact, a true connection she never felt with Geoffrey Zandieh until now, and for only this moment. He winks at her one last time and the moment is gone. Rebecca watches as the plane taxi's off into the water, then takes off and disappears into the distance. She knows that she will never see or hear from Geoffrey Zandieh again.

"You see Miss Webb, I told you Mr. Zandieh cared for you. I could tell by the way he spoke of you and now I see in the way he looks at you. We'll get you back to port. Enjoy your lunch, the ride and this beautiful day." Captain Rolle goes to the bridge as the boat is turning back toward Nassau.

The lovely lobster salad all of a sudden looks very appealing. Thick chunks of Bahamian lobster tail, avocado and tomato, the fresh aroma of lemon zest. Taking a bite, she begins to think of the conversation with Geoffrey. Did he say my friends are in Nassau? What friends? I can't wait to speak with my father and find out what this is all about. I pray that he is safe. Geoffrey didn't mention my father being in Nassau... Overwhelmed by all of the random thoughts circling around in her brain, her appetite quickly subsides.

157

The Renaissance can not cruise fast enough for Rebecca as Captain Rolle is at the helm full throttle compass header 315 degrees north west to Nassau. The waters are quite choppy now and the northeast winds, so uncommon this time of year, are swirling. In the distance Rebecca spots another seaplane coming into view. "Now what." She thinks aloud. "I hope my friend Mr. Zandieh hasn't changed his mind. Or could this be help coming for me?" She stands and walks toward the starboard side of the boat to get a better view.

The plane is flying fairly low, but doesn't appear to be landing. She watches as it does a fly by and gains altitude to make a wide turn back toward the boat. Flying too fast for her to make out who may be inside, she watches intently as the plane comes out of its turn. The sun reflects off of the lower wing causing a bright, almost blinding streak of light across the sky. Within seconds, the plane bursts into flames and explodes into a fiery ball of red. Heavy black smoke and particles fall, seemingly in slow motion toward the blue water. Rebecca screams as Captain Rolle and one of his crewmen come running toward her from the bridge.

"Miss Webb, are you alright?" The Captain rushes to her side.

She trembles violently, her body in shock. She stares out into the water watching the steam rise above where the burning seaplane made its abrupt entry into water.

"Get on 16 and alert the authorities that a seaplane just went down, give them our coordinates." The Captain yells toward the first mate. "Miss Webb, let's get you inside, we are going to get you back to Nassau as soon as possible."

"Was it Geoffrey's plane?" She asks Captain Rolle, her voice shaky.

"I don't know. I wouldn't think so. I was not expecting him to return to the boat. He did not radio us of plans to return."

* * * * *

BACK AT EXECUTIVE AIR SUPPORT, PATRIC ANXIOUSLY awaits for the conditions to improve, or for a pilot crazy enough to fly, so that a charter seaplane may become available, though the possibility is not looking good. He receives a call on his cell phone, looking at Tim he confirms who is calling. "It's Drew Webb."

"Yes sir, thanks for returning my call. The boat is called Renaissance. We tried to get a seaplane to get out there to try to locate it, but the winds are apparently too dangerous, we aren't able to secure a charter." Patric is listening very intently and shaking his head affirmatively as Tim Connelly looks on trying to figure out the details of the conversation.

"What is he saying?" Tim whispers. Patric extends his index finger asking Tim to give him a minute.

"It was so broken up sir...I couldn't tell. She didn't sound frightened or threatened, but I know she wants to be off of that boat. Sir, I'd really like to go out there with the Coast Guard if that would be possible." There is a pause and Tim begins to put the pieces together. "Thank you sir." Patric responds again to the caller. "She is a strong woman sir." Another pause. "I will wait to hear back from you." Patric ends the call and puts the phone back into his pocket.

"What's up?" Tim anxiously inquires.

"Webb is having the Coast Guard sent out there right away. They have to land and clear customs here in Nassau. They should also be able to get a pretty good idea of the location of the boat through the Bahamian customs authorities and BASRA."

"Does he know who is behind the abduction?" Tim wants more info.

"Sounds like he has a pretty good idea now. He wanted me to tell you that all of the information we left him was helpful."

159

"Sounds like you might just have your story." Patric winks.

"I need a beer. Let's get back to the marina and wait for Webb's call." Tim, feeling some sense of relief and knowing the US Coast Guard is on their way, is anxious now to get back and begin compiling his notes and putting his preliminary piece together for Bill Weller.

"Are you crazy? We've got to get Bec off that boat." Patric is insistent and determined as ever to get out there to his distressed damsel.

"I thought you just said the Coast Guard is on their way."

"Yep, and we are going with them. Webb is going to try to pull a few strings to get us on that chopper." Patric walks back to the reception desk and approaches Miss Laramore. "Excuse me again. Do you know where the US Coast Guard would fly into to clear customs?"

"Yes. They would clear at the Government Service Center, adjacent to the main commercial terminal."

"How do we get there from here?" Patric still on task.

"I can get a taxi for you if you like." Miss Laramore is happy to help.

"Please. That would be great. Thanks."

She calls for a taxi to come to the front of the building and points to the door to let the gentlemen know where the taxi would be coming to collect them.

"Are you crazy? I don't know what I ever did to deserve a best friend like you." Tim laughs but also knows his BFF is probably going to pull this off.

"Knock it off, T. We need to be there when Bec is pulled off that boat. She is going to need people that she knows and trusts out there. I am sure she is so confused at this point she has no idea who to trust."

160

"You make a great point and you are right. She will need you. You need to be there." Tim is interrupted by Miss Laramore.

"Excuse me gentlemen, your car is waiting out front to take you to customs."

Patric turns and runs toward the front door, Tim follows. They get in the cab. The driver turns around, "You goin' to the government terminal...customs?"

"Yes, as fast as possible, thanks." Feeling as though they are getting close to actually getting to Rebecca, Patric takes a deep breath and exhales into a long sigh as he leans back into the seat.

"I don't think there is any way they are going to let us on that chopper Patric." Tim is still not totally convinced.

Though Patric is not giving up. "Oh yes they are. You can use your media credentials and I am going to use Drew Webb."

"This is insane. But I'm with you buddy."

The driver slows and comes to a stop. "It is the blue building to the right."

"How much do I owe you?" Patric pulls out a wad of cash from his pants pocket.

"Ten." the driver turns around as Patric hands him a 20 dollar bill and he and Tim jump out of the car and start for the blue and white customs terminal. It is a 50 yard dash from where the taxi left them, to the entrance of the building. They rush into the office and approach the officer on duty. Streams of sweat run down the sides of both of their faces.

"Are you expecting a US Coast Guard crew to check in here this afternoon?" The officer is taken by surprise both by Patric's question and his forward manner.

"Not that I am aware of. Who are you?" The officer checks out the two gentlemen from head to toe. It is an unusual inquiry, especially from two young men who just look like another couple of American tacky tourists in Paradise. He gives them the once over, once again.

Patric calms his manner as he responds to the customs officer. "I'm sorry sir, we are to meet a US Coast Guard chopper here in Nassau when they arrive to clear."

"They would be checking in here first...however, I don't have any indication that a US Coast Guard is coming in here today." Still checking them out, the customs officer isn't going to give them any information, even if he is aware.

"Do you know where I could call to verify my information?" Insistently Patric continues to prod the officer.

"I would call whoever sent you here. Otherwise, you could check with their South Florida dispatch in Fort Pierce." The officer turns as if to tell the gentlemen that he is finished with this conversation.

"Would you happen to have that phone number?" An ever persistent Patric Taylor continues.

"I have the number. Tell me again who you are?"

"I'm sorry officer. I am Patric Taylor and this is my associate Tim Connelly. We are working with former FBI Director Drew Webb. That is who sent us here this afternoon." Tim looks at Patric as if he is crazy, but being an investigative reporter himself, he remembers some of the creative ways which he has relied on to obtain accesses.

All of a sudden the officer's attitude takes a 180 degree turn. "I know Director Webb. He used to have a home here in Nassau. I know him well. I'll be happy to make that call for you."

* * * * *

162

A BLISTERING HOT LATE SUMMER DAY IN MANHATTAN, and Maggie Pearlman and her new hot beau have arrived at 2 East 70th after a long Saturday afternoon lunch at Nello just, a few blocks away. As they stand under the awning entranceway, the doorman opens the lobby door for their entrance.

"I love a four hour lunch on a Saturday. Thanks for a wonderful afternoon." Maggie thanks her date, a little giddy from the wine.

"Shall I come in with you?" he asks. "Would be happy to walk you at least to the front door."

"Thanks, I'll be fine. I really had a great time."

"I don't think I am ready for it to end," he persists.

"Are you making a pass?" Maggie giggles.

"Respectfully, no, but I would love to continue the great conversation we were having at lunch."

"Okay, how about some coffee? Come on up. I am sure Rebecca would be thrilled for me to have you in her apartment." Maggie smiles and takes her date's arm. They continue on into the building.

"Good Evening." They greet the doorman as they walk through to the elevator with passive conversation laughing and giggling. Leaving the elevator, they stroll down the hall to Rebecca's apartment door. Maggie puts the key in the door and hesitates. "You know, I'm not sure I feel right about this. This isn't my apartment and I probably shouldn't be making myself quite so at home."

"Maggie...a cup of coffee? Come on. You already said your friend wouldn't mind. Perfectly innocent, I promise."

Maggie blushes, turns the key and opens the door. They enter to find the entire apartment ransacked, Maggie shrieks and falls to the floor.

"What the hell happened here?" The man is calm, but obviously shaken. "Maggie, are you alright?" He helps her up from the floor and supports her limp body.

"I have to do something. Call the police, something." Maggie exclaims, her body quivering from head to toe. "This is obviously not how I left the apartment this morning." Standing in the doorway they view what they can see of the apartment from this vantage point like a slow motion objective view camera. Pillows and sofa cushions thrown everywhere, paintings down off the wall, lamps turned over, rugs taken up and left in jumbled piles in the middle of the floor, drawers left open, books, magazines, papers scattered everywhere. It was ransacked alright, but who would do this to sweet Rebecca Webb and why?

"Thank goodness you were not here. Maggie, I insist that you come home with me. No monkey business, but you can not stay here. It is just not safe." His tone is somber but supportive, with obvious concern. "Come on Maggie. Close the door. Let's go downstairs and have the doorman call for the authorities. I'll stay here with you until the police arrive to file a report, and then, once again, I insist you come home with me."

"Perhaps you are right. I don't understand what happened here." Pulling the door closed, Maggie turns as the gentleman continues to support her and guide her to the elevator.

"That is for the authorities to find out. In the meantime, I will make sure that you are in good hands."

* * * * *

A BRIGHT ORANGE COAST GUARD CHOPPER makes its landing on a cleared landing pad just behind the customs building. The winds still circle at a pretty good velocity, but not too much for the powerful chopper to handle. Patric and Tim run quickly across the tarmac along with the customs officer carrying a metal covered clipboard with clearance documents. Bent over to stay under the turbulence of the propeller, they reach the chopper as the first officer welcomes Patric and Tim aboard and signs the clearance documents. The customs officer runs back toward the building and Patric and Tim are handed Coast Guard flight suits for over their clothes and a headset. The first officer helps get them buckled in as the chopper commander turns to give a thumbs up to the new passengers. They both respond in like kind and the chopper takes off.

"Welcome aboard gentlemen." The Commander's voice comes across through their headsets. "Director Webb sends his regards. We have a special mission. One of our rescue vessels was close to the area that the Renaissance was last reported, along with a Bahamian BASRA vessel. They are in the vicinity now. We've been asked to check it out, hold the yacht until the rescue vessels arrive and hopefully without any trouble, retrieve the Director's daughter from the ship and send her back to Nassau on one of the rescue vessels."

"Thank you for allowing us to go out there with you." Patric chimes in and Tim also adds, "Yes, thank you, sir."

"Director Webb felt it important enough to call in a favor for you two to be a part of this mission. We are not anticipating any problems. Sit tight, we should be underway and in the vicinity in fifteen minutes or so." The Commander turns his attention fully on the flight from Nassau over the rough, blue waters, and baron rocky islands. The view is amazing as the chopper is cruising south at optimum speed. Passing several yachts and cargo freighters, they finally come upon the Renaissance, surprisingly heading north west, back toward Nassau. The Commander initiates contact with the vessel.

"Renaissance, Renaissance, United States Coast Guard, over?"

There is no response from the Renaissance as the Commander again attempts to make contact with the yacht. "Renaissance, Renaissance, US Coast Guard Air Support, do you copy?"

"This is Renaissance, how can we be of service, sir?"

"Your vessel reported a plane going down into the water some 20 miles east of here. Rescue vessels have been deployed. Requesting permission Captain for one of our rescue vessels to come aboard to question you and your crew regarding the details of this plane crash."

Captain Rolle responds to the Chopper asking to continue on to Nassau. "We are on course into port in Nassau Harbor. Could we perhaps meet with authorities there?"

"Unfortunately Captain, it is a matter of some urgency. Please stop your vessel and prepare to anchor. Our vessel should be arriving at your coordinates in a matter of just a few minutes. Permission for them to come aboard, please." There is no response from the Renaissance as clearly, Captain Rolle is deliberating.

The Commander continues. "Captain, we have also been made aware that you may have a passenger aboard against her will. Our peaceful mission is to retrieve her from your vessel and take her home with us."

"You must be mistaken, sir." Captain Rolle calmly responds. "We have nothing of the kind. We do have a female passenger; however, she is not here against her will and we are returning her to Nassau as we speak."

"Then you won't mind if we come aboard and speak to the passenger. Please stop your engines and anchor Captain. With all due respect, if you do not stop and anchor immediately you will have a fleet of military all over your ass. I need to speak with your passenger Captain."

Rebecca, now listening intently to the conversation in the bridge, quickly makes her way to Captain Rolle's side. He begrudgingly hands her the microphone and she speaks into it clearly. "This is Rebecca Webb."

"Miss Webb, are you alright?"

"Yes sir, I am fine, but I am ready to get off this boat."

"Hang tight Miss Webb, we'll have you off of there in no time." The chopper commander signs off and turns communication over to the ground crew.

In the meantime the US Coast Guard and BASRA vessels reach the Renaissance cruising on both sides of the yacht with their sirens blaring. Captain Rolle brings his ship to an idle position and prepares to drop anchor. Rebecca patiently watches, now knowing that these boats are here to take her home and not here only to respond to the seaplane crash. She runs out of the boat to the stern as the Coast Guard vessel ties up to the Renaissance and the crew helps a couple of the officers aboard.

An anxiously excited Patric Taylor, who has been listening to the radio correspondence, looks down onto the Renaissance and sees Rebecca standing on the stern, her arms crossed and hands rubbing her arms as if she is chilled. "Sir, can you get me down onto one of those boats? I need to get down there with Rebecca. Tim?"

"Oh buddy, you don't think I'm going to..." Looking down to the water from his window, Tim's face turns green. Patric laughs, "No, man. I'll see you back at the marina...Commander?"

"I'll get you down there son."

Patric takes off his headset as the first officer goes to the back of the chopper and returns with hoisting equipment and harness.

By this point, the Coast Guard officers on the ground are escorting Rebecca and her belongings off of the Renaissance and on to the Coast Guard transport boat. All harnessed up, and on the most important mission of his life, Patric is lowered from the chopper onto the boat. Carefully, one of the officers grabs him as his body sways in the wind and pulls him safely onto the boat. They release the harness and as it flies back up to the chopper, the Commander gives Patric a thumbs up and Patric waves. The chopper turns forming a whirlpool of waves with it's power in the water below and accelerates away from the boat. Not really paying attention to the handsome man in the Coast Guard flight suit, Rebecca suddenly feels his presence. She looks toward the man and screams.

"Oh my God, Patric! What are you doing here? I knew I called the right person, but how...?" Before she could finish, he runs to her and they embrace so tightly neither one can barely breath.

"Hey babe, just dropped in to see how you were doing." His voice is like a calm breeze echoing directly into her ear.

With a huge smile, and tears flowing uncontrollably down her beautiful cheeks she looks at him, "Boy, are you a sight for sore eyes."

One of the crew hands Patric a large orange blanket and he gingerly wraps it around Rebecca. "God you are so beautiful."

Her tears now turn into laughter, knowing that she has probably never looked worse than she does at this moment, but also knowing that it doesn't matter. All that matters is that she is safe and somehow, with a miracle from the heavens above, she is in the arms of the man that she loves, has always loved and always will. "I am sure you have a lot to tell me...like how in the world you got here."

Her windblown and tangled hair is glued to her face by the remnants of the tears as Patric tries gently to move it away from her eyes. "Bec, I am so glad to see you. I am sure you have a lot to tell me too."

The day has turned to evening and the sun begins to make its peaceful descent from the deep blue sky into the deep blue ocean below. A nearly blinding bright yellow glare guides the Coast Guard transport vessel as it makes its way due west towards Nassau. It is as if the streak of light is providing a roadmap for their journey back to Nassau and safe harbor.

Rebecca and Patric turn back to watch as the BASRA (Bahamas Air Sea Rescue) vessel seizes the Renaissance which it will escort back to port for questioning. Rebecca thinks about Captain Rolle and his crew, how nice they were to her in the worst of circumstances, and wonders what may become of them.

No more words are spoken as the two stand in full embrace on the bow. The yellow glare of the sun begins its transformation to a brilliant orange glow on the deep turquoise water. It is simply breathtaking. For just a moment, she closes her eyes and has no memory of the previous 48 hours. She feels only the warmth of the setting sun, the strong embracing arms around her and the gentle bliss of where she is in this moment. For just this moment, all is right with the world.

* * * * *

THE EARLY EVENING SKY TURNS TO DUSK, though the lights of the Coast Guard vessel are easily seen approaching the dock at Hurricane Hole Marina. A very anxious Drew Webb awaits to greet his daughter with his friend, Leslie March at his side. Tim Connelly also stands waiting, chatting with 2 FBI Officers who are on the case, dressed in stock black boilerplate suits with military haircuts. Both Tim and the officers are careful at this point not to share too much information as typically journalists and FBI Agents have little trust for, or interest in, one another beyond what is necessary. They always seem to be on different sides of the same side. One side, that of protecting a story and one side of telling it.

The officers meet the boat at the dock and as the bow thrusters send it dockside, they assist the Coast Guard crew in tying it down. Drew rushes to his daughter and Patric helps her off the boat.

"Rebecca, I am so sorry. I had no idea something like this could or would happen. I just never saw the connection here until it was too late." He hugs his daughter tightly with joy. She is back on solid ground and safely in his arms.

"Daddy, what is going on? What are you involved in? I asked Patric to explain, but he insisted that I hear everything directly from you."

"My darling, I am so sorry. The important thing now is that you are here and safe. We have plenty of time to catch up on the details, and I promise you I will share everything with you, but don't worry, you can not and will not be harmed again. Please forgive your old man for not protecting you better than this." Patric stands off in the background while Rebecca reunites with her father. What he really wants to do is to whisk her off on the Mer Soleil, just the two of them to a deserted island never to be seen or heard from again, but as reality would kill another great idea...of course this is not possible. Drew looks past Rebecca and extends his right arm to shake Patric's hand.

"How can I ever thank you Patric. I appreciate..."

Shaking Drew's hand firmly Patric interupts, "My pleasure, sir. I am just happy to have our girl back, and on safe ground."

"Mr. Director, sir," the FBI Officer interjects. "I am sorry to interrupt this happy reunion but we do need to speak with your daughter, sir."

"I understand, of course." Drew's tone changes.

"Miss Webb, could we take you with us for a few questions?"

"I don't think I will be of much help, but of course I am happy to cooperate. Can my father and Patric be there as well?" At this point, Rebecca doesn't want to be without the security of both of these important men in her life by her side.

"I'd like to be included also." Making his way into the conversation, Tim knows that Rebecca has yet to realize that he was here.

"Oh, Tim. I didn't even see you there. It's been sort of a stressful day. What are you doing here? God, I'm confused."

"To say the least I am sure...on both counts! Hey Bec. Glad you're okay." Tim blushes as Rebecca reaches over to give him a hug and kiss on the cheek.

"I can't wait to hear how you two got involved in all of this, but thanks, thanks so much." The lump in her throat is obvious, as Rebecca begins to get a little teary eyed, the FBI Officer takes control.

"It is not possible, nor appropriate to include a newspaper reporter in this interview. Now if we can proceed?"

"But..." Tim begins to make a case but is quickly interrupted by Drew Webb. "Of course officer, we do understand." Looking at Tim with an apologetic half smile and affirmative nod, reassuring Tim that he will get the information that he seeking in due time.

"Director Webb, if you would like to sit in, that would be fine, but I'll have to draw the line there."

Rebecca looks at Patric with those beautiful puppy dog eyes in disappointment. Now that she finally has him, what appears to be, back in her life, she doesn't want to leave his side for even a moment. Things seem to be moving so quickly and out of control right now as her head begins to spin.

"Bec, go ahead. It's okay. I'll catch up with you later." Patric sees the fear and uncertainty in her eyes and tries to ease her anxiety.

"When?" she asks immediately, without thought or hesitation.

"When you finish up here. Call me on my mobile. I'm not going anywhere. You have the number." Winking at her, she feels her legs getting weak like string beans in boiling water.

"Yes I do and thank God for that! I'll call you soon." She reaches for Patric's hand and squeezes it as hard as she can, then gives him a flirty wink. Smiling right back at her, he gives her hand a squeeze and let's go. Rebecca walks towards her father and they follow the FBI Officers. Patric never takes his eyes off of her as she walks away, his heart pounding, what feels like 1000 beats per minute.

"Daddy, are we staying here tonight?"

"Yes my darling. I have a villa at the Ocean Club for all of us, very safe with generous FBI protection. I thought we'd have a little celebration dinner later there if you are up to it." Drew turns to Leslie. "Les, why don't you take Patric and Tim back to the hotel with you and Rebecca and I will join you as soon as we finish up here. You gentlemen will join us I hope?"

"Thank you, sir, yes, I would be honored." Patric immediately answers without cause or hesitation.

"Yes, thanks, of course I will." Tim responds affirmatively as well.

"Tim, we'll work on that story of yours when the time is right. Let's get the details in order and let the FBI do their job. They are on the way to Cuba as we speak and no one is aware of their mission. I will have first hand information, and the story will be yours when it is time to release it."

"Thank you, sir. I really appreciate that."

"Okay, I guess I will see you all at the Ocean Club in a little while. Leslie, thanks so much for helping my dad get through this. I know he appreciates your support." Now relaxed a bit, knowing that everyone is to be together soon, Rebecca is ready to work with the officers and get this nightmare behind her.

"We are just glad you are safe Rebecca." Leslie takes Drew's hand and with a respectful nod, he tells her it is time for her to go.

The FBI Officer clears his throat, somewhat loudly in order to get everyone's attention, and tries to takes control of this situation once and for all. "If that is all, then perhaps we can proceed?" The group disassembles to go in their respective directions when Tim's cell phone rings.

"Hi honey. Yes, Becca is here and safe and everything is great. I will be home tomorrow." As the color begins to leave Tim's face, everyone stops almost knowingly what is about to happen next. "Now? But it's not time yet. You are going to have to wait until I get there." There is a pause. "I have no idea, but just hang in there for a few hours please!!!! I am on my way. I love you." Tim looks around at everyone. "I'm sorry, the baby is coming early, premature, I've got to get back to New York. Oh my God, I'm having a son...now!"

"Tim, take my airplane." Drew offers. "I'll call the pilots right away and have them file a flight plan. By the time you get to the airport, they will be ready for wheels up. For God's sake son, get yourself home."

"I can't thank you enough, sir. This could be my only chance of making it in time." Frozen in his steps, Tim can't move. His body rigid, his legs heavy.

"Just go, son. Get in a taxi and go!" Dialing his phone, Webb prepares his pilots for their change of plans.

"T, get your ass out of here." Patric gives him a gentle shove and Tim finally starts quickly toward to the marina office.

"Good luck, Tim. Give Maureen our love!" Rebecca shouts to him as he runs through the marina office.

"Director Webb." the FBI Officer sternly tries again to take control.

"Yes...Rebecca, we need to..."

She interrupts, "I'm ready Daddy. I can't wait to get this over with, have a long hot shower and be with my family and best friends."

They follow the officers now, finally, into a black sedan waiting at the marina entrance. "I know baby, we are almost there. I promise, nothing like this will ever happen to you again. I am so thankful that God brought you back to us safely."

Left are Leslie and Patric still on the dock. "We haven't been formally introduced as yet, I'm Leslie. I've heard so much about you Patric." She gently touches his arm in a motherly and comforting sort of way.

"It is very nice to meet you Leslie. I hope some of what you heard about me was good." He smiles.

"Oh, I think you may be surprised just how so. Let's get a car back to the Ocean Club and wait for Drew and Rebecca. I am sure you must be exhausted."

"Yes. It has been a very long day. I am just so glad it is over and Bec is safe. I've been crazy worrying about that woman these past days."

"It is obvious that you care for Rebecca very much."

"Yes. Yes I do. Let me get a car for you to the hotel. I need to clean up a bit on my boat here and I'll meet all of you at the Ocean Club later. After Bec is back there and has had a chance to rest and feeling up to the company, would you have her give me a call?"

"I am sure that will be sooner rather than later. I'll let her know. I look forward to talking with you more later this evening." With another soft motherly pat on his shoulder Leslie adds, "I can get my own car. You go on back to your boat and get some rest."

He smiles and nods, turning back to the docks and the Mer Soleil. The sun has fully disappeared now but the entire sky still radiant in a deep red glow. The stars are beginning to sparkle very brightly amidst the fiery background. Patric reaches in the cooler on the deck and pulls out a cold Kalik, reflecting on the day. Offering a toast up toward the sky, he lifts his bottle high and looks to the heavens. "Thank you," and a tear streams down his chiseled cheek.

Just then, Patric's cell phone rings and snaps him back from the stars. Still a bit choked up, he answers. "Hey."

"It's me man. I'm getting ready to take off but I just wanted to say that I'm glad about you and Becca. It is the way things are supposed to be, you know?" You can hear the smile in Tim's voice.

"What are you talking about? We just did what we had to do for a friend. By the way, thanks for hanging in there with me padze. I owe you one." Patric takes a long deserved gulp of beer.

"I don't have time to argue with your stubborn ass right now, because I've got to get home and have a kid. Just take care of her, okay?"

"Get your ass home and call me as soon as you know something. I hope you make it in time. I am sure everything will be fine."

175

"I'm a little worried, about the premie thing, but I know my son is strong and even though he is coming early..." Tim pauses and becomes a little choked up himself. "You just go enjoy the evening with your girl. She IS your girl, my friend."

Tim has known Patric much too long not to speak what's on his mind, and what he knows is true. He has never been one to beat around the bush anyway, and of course, always felt that his two dear friends belonged together, and that one day, would come to finding their way back where they belong.

"Thanks for everything Timbo. We'll get your story."

"What a day!...later..." Tim disconnects and turns off his phone for take off. He leans back in the seat, eyes closed still holding the phone in his lap. "I'm on my way Mo," he says quietly to himself.

* * * * *

CHAPTER FIFTEEN

SEATED AROUND A SMALL CONFERENCE TABLE at the American Embassy in downtown Nassau, Rebecca and her father the former FBI director, and the two FBI Officers who brought them in, meet. One officer is seated, legal pad on the table in front of him, as the second officer leans forward on the conference table, his hands folded on the table in front of him.

"Miss Webb, we have not been formally introduced, I am Officer Ramsey."

"Rebecca, please call me Rebecca." She gracefully informally introduces herself.

"Rebecca, I know this has been a very difficult few days for you, but if you could just bear with us for a few questions." Officer Ramsey looks at Rebecca solemnly, almost to look straight through her. She nods. "Can you tell us more about the man who abducted you." He looks over at the notes on his partner's legal pad. "A Mr. Zandieh?" Rebecca nods again. "Do you know this man's business? Did he ever discuss why you were abducted?"

"He was always very vague. He described himself as an international broker of sorts. Basically he didn't tell me much of anything. I've known him for only a few months. He came to me for an investment portfolio and as I have many very wealthy clients who don't always share the intimate details of the source of their funds and assets, I didn't find his illusiveness unusual, really." She becomes a little upset and teary. "Was it he that was aboard the seaplane that crashed into the ocean?" Reaching in his pocket, her father hands her his hankerchief. "Thanks, Daddy."

"Our men are assisting the Bahamian authorities at the crash site. BASRA has confirmed that there were two souls on board, one pilot and one passenger. There were no survivors." Ramsey adds.

Rebecca now very shaken, "I know. It was obvious that no one could have survived. What was the cause of the explosion?"

"It is still under investigation. We have not received any word as yet. Had Zandieh been on the Renaissance?"

"Yes. He had just been there earlier in the afternoon," trying to pull herself together. "I'm sorry."

"I know this is difficult." Officer Ramsey trying to console her.

"He came there to tell me that I was free, he was letting me go. He apparently couldn't go through with it and instructed Captain Rolle, the captain, to bring me back to Nassau. I don't understand what any of this is about."

"He was letting you go?" Asks Officer Ramsey.

"Yes, that is what he said." She blots the tears from under her eyes.

"Did he mention anything that would give you an idea as to what his orders actually were or who they were coming from?"

"No. He only said that my father could tell me when I got back to New York." She looks at her father and he takes her hand in both of his. The strain that he is under as he watches his daughter go through this interrogation is almost more than the former director can handle, though it was his business for so many years. What a different scenario when it involves one of your own.

"Why did he say he was letting you go?"

"He said he didn't have any use for me anymore." She begins to cry again. "He told me that he had cared for me and..."

"I know this is difficult Miss Webb, excuse me, Rebecca, but do you have any idea from whom he was receiving these orders?" Ramsey persists as Rebecca does her best to gather her thoughts.

"I am sorry Officer Ramsey, I really am not of much help. I really don't know anything. I wish I did, I wish I could help." She looks once again at her father. "All I remember is having one glass of champagne at the Ocean Club and my next recollection is waking up alone in a stateroom on the Renaissance heading to parts unknown." Rebecca pauses, like a light bulb has just lit in a very dark memory. "Wait a minute. I do remember something. He was seated next to me in that stateroom, I must have been sleeping still because I don't remember seeing him, but I do vaguely remember over hearing a phone conversation he was having and I am fairly certain he mentioned the White House...yes, I heard *vice president*."

"The White House ma'am?" The Officer is stunned and needing clarification.

"Yes. I'm certain of it now. I don't think I was dreaming." Rebecca looks back at Officer Ramsey. Her mind is clear now as if the cobwebs left behind by the small amount of anesthesia still left in her system have disappeared. "If it makes any difference, the captain and crew of the Renaissance were very good to me."

"Except for the fact that they were holding you captive, against you will." Ramsey adds.

"Well, yes...except for that. What will happen to them?"

"There will be ramifications. The vessel has, of course, been seized and they are all being held for questioning. If they help the investigation, the penalties may be negotiable."

"Is there anything else Officer Ramsey? I am very tired." Rebecca leans back to stretch, closes her eyes and shifts her shoulders from side to side stretching her neck. Her father feels it is time for him to get involved in the conversation.

"Gentlemen, may I take her back to the hotel now? If you need anything further, of course, we will be available to you at any time."

"Yes sir, of course." Ramsey responds to the former director and turns to Rebecca. "I am glad you are safe, Rebecca. Director Webb, thanks for your assistance with this. I will be in touch when we hear from Cuba." He pauses for a moment and refers again to Rebecca. "There is one more thing. If you know the cell phone number that Zandieh would have been using, we could possibly trace that phone call."

"Hmmm. Gosh, I am sorry I don't. If it is the same number that he would use to call and text me, it would be in my cell phone; but, it is dead at the moment. It should be in my bag. Did someone get my bag off the boat? I haven't even thought about that."

Looking at the other officer who has remained silent to this point, only taking a few notes Ramsey asks, "Do we have her bag?" The other officer nods and leaves the room for a moment.

"You are welcome to keep my phone if it helps. I gave his business card to Tim Connelly some time ago. The cell number would be on it as well. My assistant could also retrieve all of his contact information from his file in my office on Monday morning." Feeling that all of this could be of some help, possibly leading to exactly what Geoffrey's mission and intentions were, Rebecca feels a sense of relief as if she is actually helping now in some way.

The second officer returns to the conference room with Rebecca's travel bag and hand bag and lays them, not so gently, on the conference table. "May I?" asks Ramsey pointing at her bags.

"Of course...sure." My phone should be in the handbag.

Ramsey again looks at the second officer who nods. It is quite obvious that the FBI has already thoroughly gone through Rebecca's things. Suddenly she feels degraded, her privacy invaded. For a moment it makes her feel even worse than Geoffrey's abduction of her. At least he was always respectful, she thought.

And to think she just gave them permission, but somewhat after the fact. Officer Ramsey hands Rebecca her handbag. "Thank you." She reaches inside and hands him her cell phone.

"Thanks. We will need to keep your phone during the course of the investigation. It will be used as evidence. Could you also provide us with your assistant's information so that we can contact her on Monday morning?" Ramsey slides the legal pad across the conference table to her along with a pencil.

"Of course." She calmly obliges, but at this point, has really had enough FBI manners, or lack thereof, to last a while.

"If there isn't anything else, I'd really like to get my little girl back to the hotel to rest. I will look forward to hearing from you when you learn more."

"With all due respect, most will be classified sir, but we will report back as much as we are able to." Ramsey with his not so kind FBI manners on.

"I am aware of the circumstances and procedure. I will discuss with Director Mueller my need for clearance. Thank you gentlemen." Reminding Officer Ramsey exactly who he is trying to insult, Drew Webb makes his point very clear.

"Of course, sir." Ramsey responds, obviously put back in his position by the former director as only he could do.

"Are you ready honey?" Drew Webb stands and helps his daughter up and to the exit. "You know where to find us if you need to."

"Yes. Thank you sir. How long will you be staying in Nassau?"

"I think we will probably be leaving to return to New York tomorrow." Drew and Rebecca continue towards the Embassy exit.

"Very well sir."

Leaving the building where the black sedan awaits to take them back to Paradise Island and the Ocean Club, the two get into the back seat of the car. Rebecca puts her travel bag on the floor of the car and her handbag lays next to her beside the car door. "I'd better call Patric and let him know we are on our way back. May I use your phone Daddy?"

"Are you sure you are up to that this evening? Perhaps you need some rest right now." A concerned and protective father appears and though Rebecca knows he has only her best interest at heart, the one thing that she does need right now, is Patric Taylor.

"You might be right Daddy, but I really do want to see Patric. I'd love for the four of us to just have a very quiet dinner. Not a terribly late night. Is that okay?"

How can her father say no at this point as he sympathetically hands her his cell phone. "Of course Rebecca. You can have anything that you want." With the biggest smile he has seen from his daughter in some time she begins to dial.

"Hi...how are you?" In her most innocent but sultry voice.

On the other end of the phone line, a smile equally as big. "Much better now. Are you finished with the FBI?"

"I am afraid I wasn't much help to them, but we are headed back to the Ocean Club. Are you there with Leslie?"

"No. I came back to the boat for a shower."

"I can't wait to have a long one myself. Would you come over and have dinner with us?" Rebecca trying not to seem presumptuous.

"Are you sure you are feeling like company?"

"Please come. I would love to see you, then I will have everything that I need with you guys with me," winking at her Dad. "Bye."

Handing the phone back to her father, her hands clammy, her arms weak. "He really is a good man, Daddy."

"Yes, he is Rebecca. The best."

She looks at her father a bit puzzled and then smiles. Drew puts his arm around his daughter and her weak body falls toward him as she lays her head on his shoulder and releases a huge sigh. She wants to ask questions, get answers, try to understand, but her body is too weak, her mind too exhausted and all she can think of right now, is Patric. The sedan drives over the bridge to Paradise Island as she gently falls asleep on her father's soft shoulder.

* * * * *

SEVERAL VERY DARK MILITARY HELICOPTERS surround the beautiful Cuban Estate near Guantanamo Bay, on this very clear, very dark night. No sirens, no lights, they land at various vantage points both to the front lawn and rear of the property. Special forces operatives storm the property. Every entrance, exit, window is covered. On signal, they enter to find the entire property desolately empty.

A dark sedan with no lights enters the drive and proceeds to the front entranceway. Special Ops Officers open the front door and three black-suited gentlemen exit the car and enter the estate.

They are greeted by one of the special ops officers. "The building is empty sir. It looks like we didn't miss them by much. There was definitely someone here in the past 12 hours."

"Shake the place down. I want to examine every hair, every piece of dust in this place. Get it done and get everyone out of here as quickly and quietly as you got in."

"Affirmative, sir," the special ops officer turns and returns to the building.

Turning to the other suits, "Fuck. Can you believe we missed the mother fucker again?" He dials his phone. "Sir, the building is empty sir. Yes. I will follow up." Throwing the phone to the ground. "FUCK! We need to call Nassau and let them know what we've found."

They continue in, walking through the estate as the special operations officers quickly and diligently gather their evidence. Walking through the open veranda doors leading out to the ocean they notice that there are still half empty drinking glasses on a table. Whoever was here obviously left in a hurry, and obviously had some warning.

* * * * *

CHAPTER SIXTEEN

A FRANTIC EXPECTANT FATHER RUNS THROUGH the corridor at St. Luke's Roosevelt Hospital's Women's Health and Birthing Center. "Connelly," screaming at the top of his lungs, Tim desperately wants to find his hopefully still pregnant wife. The facility at 1000 10th Avenue is amazing, he knows Maureen is in the best of care but still hoping to be at her side prior to the arrival of their impending bundle of joy.

"Where is Maureen Connelly?" He arrives at the nurses' station, soaking wet with sweat, straight from Millionaire FBO in Teterboro where his flight from Nassau landed...what seems like a lifetime ago. "I am the father. Where is my wife? Am I too late?"

"Calm down Mr. Connelly." The nurse stands, walks around to the front side of the nurses' station desk. "She's had a bit of a tough time, but you're not too late. That baby must be waiting for you. Let's get you suited up. Follow me, Mr. Connelly."

"Suited up? What have I got to do?"

"Have a baby, Mr. Connelly, or at least help your wife have a baby. It's not so bad."

"After what I've been through the past 48 hours, this should be a piece of cake." Tim follows the nurse down the hall where she hands him a set of Kelly green scrubs. They continue down the corridor as Tim tries to walk and pull his uniform over his very wet sweaty clothing at the same time. Entering the birthing room where a patient, Maureen Connelly waits for her man. Tim pulls the mask up over his face.

"Tim, thank God you made it. Thanks for getting here, honey. I told everyone that he was going to wait for you." Maureen is obviously in pain, but also quite relaxed and calm.

"I wouldn't have missed it for anything, Mo." Tim rushes to her side and takes her hand. The nurse rolls her eyes, then smiles.

"Is Rebecca alright?" Maureen speaks softly and though concerned for their dear friend, she is obviously feeling uncomfortable at this point.

"All is well with the world, sweetie. Now let's have a son." Squeezing Maureen's hand, and with a wink and a smile, Tim gives his wife a nod.

Maureen's OB/GYN, enters the room, quite hurriedly as the nurse hands her Maureen's chart. "Glad you could join us Mr. Connelly." She looks up and passes Maureen chart back to the nurse.

"Me too. We weren't expecting this to happen for a while." The doctor notices Tim's face becoming pale. There is a pit in his stomach, his entire body becomes numb, his head light as a feather.

"Well, now that you are here, maybe this little guy will make his way into the world and say hello to his mom and dad. Nurse?"

Tim takes his wife's hand very tightly as things begin to get started.

The doctor takes position and looks up to Maureen. "Okay Maureen, let's give it a push..."

* * * * *

A SIMPLY GORGEOUS EVENING IN PARADISE, as Drew Webb and his friend Leslie admire the incredible view. A table is set for four on the terrace of their villa overlooking a lighted infinity edge pool that appears to cascade directly into the turquoise ocean. Spotlights light up the ocean and glimmer on palms as they sway in the breeze as if they were themselves dancing in celebration. Candlelight warms the white linen tablecloth and tropical flowers add vibrant color to it's canvas. The sound of the waves crashing onto the surf in the distance and the distant sound of music coming from the Dune Bar at the Ocean Club provide background entertainment.

"Looking at this most amazing site, it is hard to believe what you have been through these past days." With a compassionate look, Leslie takes Drew's hand.

"Isn't this just heaven. I had almost forgotten what a magical place this is. I am just so elated to have my baby girl back and safe."

"I know you can't tell me entirely what this is all about, but I am so happy to be here with you to celebrate Rebecca's safety. Thanks for including me, Drew. It is very special. I only hope that I have been of some comfort for you."

"Oh Leslie, I can't thank you enough for being here with me. Your support has meant so much these past few days." Drew pulls Leslie's hand to his mouth and gently kisses the back of her hand, looking still straight ahead towards the ocean. The villa's doorbell rings and Rebecca comes dashing out of her bedroom looking absolutely amazing, especially considering her ordeal.

"I'll get it. It's probably Patric." Rebecca runs toward the door with small and excited steps like those of a ballerina dancing across a stage. Drew and Leslie look at each other and smile. As Rebecca opens the door, beside the FBI agent who is posted to the door, she sees him, the ever handsome Patric Taylor, holding a beautiful bright pink hibiscus bloom.

187

As if there were no one else in the world, but the two of them, he hands her the flower. "Wow," is all he can say, as she literally takes his breath away.

"Oh, stop. You are looking pretty damn hot yourself." They kiss, then she escorts him out to the terrace by his hand. "Isn't this beautiful?"

"Leslie, Judge Webb." Greeting the hosts, Patric reaches out his hand in jesture. Drew grabs a hold of Patric's hand and pulls him in for a big bear hug, patting him on the back.

"Glad you could join us, son." Drew steps back and smiles.

"Thank you sir." Patric looks at Rebecca with bewilderment and gives her a wink.

"The butler should be back anytime with dinner. I know you must be starving. Patric, I hope it is okay, Rebecca insisted on ordering for you." Leslie says as she winks at Rebecca.

"That's terrific," He laughs. "I think she pretty much knows what I would like."

Drew hands everyone a glass of champagne. "I know how you are feeling about champagne right now darling, but how about joining your old man for just one toast?" She takes the glass and nods affirmatively. "To Rebecca. My strong and amazing daughter. We are so glad you are safe, princess. And to Patric, thanks for all you have done to help get my little girl out of harm's way. Leslie, thanks for being here for me." He holds up his glass. "And to this lovely family celebration. Cheers!"

It is quite amazing really, that when the fear or pain of a traumatic time in one's life seems to be past, the distance between then and now grows at an exponentially rapid pace.

"Daddy, when are you going to be able to tell me what this has all been about? Don't you think I have a right to know?"

"It's classified, Rebecca. In due time, I will share every single detail, but for now, I want you to rest, relax and enjoy this evening."

"What...do you think I am going to tell someone?" She adds sarcastically.

"As I said, in due time. I'm not totally certain myself at the moment to be honest, but as soon as I have the full and complete details, I will share and explain everything to you." Drew is interrupted by the doorbell.

"That must be our dinner." Leslie scurries to the door to help the butler deliver their food.

"I'll help. I am starving!" Rebecca follows closely behind Leslie as they leave the terrace and walk through the villa to answer the door.

"Dead end?" Patric turns to Drew.

"The son of a bitch was gone. Without a trace, as yet anyway. Perhaps they'll find something. I don't know. How did he...and within hours?"

"What happens now?" Patric asks.

The girls make their way back out to the terrace with the butler and a cart stacked high with silver plate covers. The butler proceeds in arranging the food on the table.

"What are you two plotting out here?" Pointing her finger at both men, Rebecca can tell that whatever it was that they were discussing, it wasn't going to continue in front of her and Leslie.

"No plotting, just celebrating having our girl back with us where she belongs." Patric's speaks before he even realized what he said.

The four are seated and begin enjoying this most delightful dinner, laughing, toasting. Drew watches the interaction between his daughter and Patric. Though they have not been together in some time, he sees their connection to one another and feels their deep love. He senses the foundation of this love, in their un-abiding friendship and trust. The warm feeling of a parent, seeing their child who has already come unto their own, happy, truly happy and in love. A hopeless romantic himself, it only makes this proud father even more proud. As the celebration continues, there is knock at the door.

"I told them we did not want to be disturbed. Excuse me for a moment." Drew gets up to handle the interruption.

"Let me go, Drew. You stay here with Rebecca and Patric." Leslie says as she gets up.

"Thanks Les. Could you please tell the agent again that we don't want to be disturbed."

Leslie walks through the villa and leaves the three alone on the terrace. Rebecca gently places her hand on her father's shoulder. "You two seem to be getting on very well Dad. I really am fond of her and so glad she was able to be here for you."

Leslie returns to the table, accompanied by FBI Officer Ramsey and his side kick, Officer King. "I'm sorry Drew, they insisted." Leslie obviously upset by the intrusion.

"Gentlemen, is this something that can wait until tomorrow perhaps?" Drew stands and addresses the officers.

"Unfortunately not, sir. And do pardon the interruption of your reunion with your daughter, but we are going to have to ask you to come with us."

"What? Now? At this time of night?" Drew isn't going anywhere, or at least he doesn't want to.

"I am sorry sir. Please don't make this more difficult than it already is." Officer Ramsey is apologetic in his tone, but perfectly serious.

"What is this? What is going on?"

"We have been instructed to take you into custody. Protective custody, but you must come with us, sir. Now."

"Custody? What are you talking about?" Very upset, Rebecca now stands questioning the officers.

"I am not at liberty to say ma'am, but Director Webb, if you could please come with us. We have our orders."

"I am not sure who your orders are coming from, but of course I will cooperate." Drew prepares to leave with the officers.

"Daddy. This isn't right." Rebecca exclaims.

"It's okay baby. Let me go with these gentlemen and get this straightened out. You are in good hands here." Drew winks at Patric. "You all enjoy the rest of the evening. I'm sure you will all be ready to turn in soon anyway. If I don't make it back here tonight, I will see you all back in New York tomorrow. Patric, could I entrust you to see that these two incredible ladies get safely back to the city tomorrow? I have made all of the arrangements. My plane will be at Executive FBO in the morning."

"Of course sir. It would be my pleasure. Is there anything else I can do for you?" Patric only too happy to oblige.

"No. Thanks Patric. I'll be fine and we will resume this celebration at home very soon." Moving toward the villa door with the officers, Drew turns to blow a kiss to both Leslie and his daughter.

"Daddy, I don't understand?"

"Let me work with these gentlemen, I'll get to the bottom of it."

"I promise everything will be fine. Leslie, I am sorry to have to leave you prematurely. Thanks for everything this week. I'll call you as soon as I get home." Drew turns back kissing Leslie on the cheek.

"Be safe," she whispers into his ear.

Rebecca rushes to hug her father and as she lets go and stands back, he turns to leave with the officers. He walks through the villa, collecting his briefcase and a couple of personal items. As the door closes, it is as if this whole tumultuous situation has returned. Their wonderful celebration taken from them in an instant. Feeling like they have just been kicked in the stomach, no one feels the desire to take another bite. There is silence now, only the sound of the distant waves along the shore.

Leslie rises from her seat. "You two must be absolutely exhausted and I am a little tired myself. Would you two mind if I left you alone and call it a night?"

"Of course not. I am not far behind you." Rebecca reaches out her hand to Leslie. They give each other a squeeze.

"Good night. See you in the morning. Sleep well." Leslie strolls back into the villa and disappears into her room.

"She is so lovely. I am so happy she was such a support to my dad through this."

"Bec, you have got to be exhausted. Why don't you try to get some sleep. I'll see you in the morning." Getting up from his seat, Patric takes Rebecca's hand and helps her up, guiding her inside the villa. He closes and locks the doors behind him.

Rebecca stops and with her lovely pouty and demure eyes, "Won't you stay here tonight? With me? I don't think I could get any sleep lying here alone. I wouldn't feel safe. Anyway, no big deal, but I would love for you stay." Need she say more? The eyes already had him.

IT IS A VERY WINDY DAY IN LOWER MANHATTAN, as summer begins it's journey's end. And what a summer it has been. An elevator door opens, Rebecca, holding Patric's hand in one, takes a moment to smell the fresh flowers in her other hand. They enter the corridor at St. Luke's Roosevelt leading toward Maureen Connelly's room. Hand in hand they peek into the room marked "Connelly." The streaming sunlight coming through the window is almost blinding, but through the dust-filled light, a young mother holds her new son, surrounded by beautiful flowers in every color of the rainbow. Father Tim is seated closely by her side.

Rebecca and Patric tiptoe into the room. "What a gorgeous family." Rebecca smiles with delight. She walks toward the bed and hands the fresh bouquet of freshly cut white roses, tulips, daisies and wild flowers to Tim, donning him with a kiss on the cheek, then reaches over to hug Maureen and baby Connelly. "Congratulations."

Patric, following directly behind her shakes his best friend's hand. "Congrats Padze. I am not going to kiss you, but I did smuggle us a couple of Cubans. I'm proud of you my man." Patric reaches in his shirt pocket handing Tim one of the cigars with a playful wink.

"Cristo II, not bad. You've always had good taste my friend. Thanks." Tim immediately gives the Cuban treasure a sniff and then places it between his teeth and lips. Patric takes his cigar as you would a glass of champagne and gestures a toast to his friend. Following in like kind he also takes the aromatic stogie into his mouth.

Tim, speaking as best he can with a cigar in his mouth, makes the formal introduction. "Meet Timothy Patrick Connelly. It's an old family name." He looks at Patric and nods.

"Hey buddy. I look forward to growing up with you." Patric looking into the eyes of Timothy Patrick, puts his arm around Rebecca and pulls her close. "You look just like your beautiful mama, thank God. And how is mama? Mo how ya doin'?"

"Doing great. Thanks for coming by you two. How are YOU doing? Tim has been filling me on what you all have been through. Rebecca, I am so …"

Rebecca interrupts, "It's okay Maureen. I am worried about my father, but he seems to be on top of everything. Hey, this is nothing compared to what you've just been through. I can't even imagine." Rebecca looks at the baby and tickles his chest. "He is just perfect."

"Isn't he beautiful?" Maureen also admiring her newborn son.

"Why would you call a man beautiful? What's wrong with you women. He is a handsome hunk of Connelly, and brother," looking at Patric, "you should see his…"

Maureen abruptly interrupts her husband. "Is that all you guys think about?"

"Well…" Tim laughs and the others join.

"It is so great seeing you two together. Tim told me everyone was okay and then said…all is right with the world. I think I know now exactly what he meant." Maureen smiles as she reaches for Rebecca's hand with her free hand.

"Hey, we are just happy to see the three of you, healthy, happy and terrific. Sorry we kept the old man from almost missing the little guy's arrival." Apologetically Patric adds his sentiments. The girls start having baby talk among themselves and guys migrate out into the hallway for a moment.

"Have you heard from Webb?"

"Only briefly, like Bec said, he seems to be on top of everything, but no details as yet. I still can't believe the son of a bitch had already vanished when they got to Cuba. Have you heard anything on your end at the paper? I know Webb has been in touch with Weller."

"Weller is also pretty tight lipped, but confidentially told me that Drew Webb, being involved early on with the administration, and the bin Laden situation, felt their intentions were less than honorable from the beginning and that part of this was to try to keep Gitmo open after the new administration takes over. He feels there are those who may have sold him out because of his ideas and suspicions which may have led to Becca's abduction, somehow, but again, no details, he has asked me also to remain tight lipped until we have verification of the missing links to report. Weller has my story, but he is waiting for Webb's verification of the facts before it goes to print. When you could be implying a connection with members of the administration, your facts better be 100% accurate."

"You are fucking kidding me. So, there definitely is a link to DC? This is un-fucking-believable. I hope Webb is protected through this. He has really put everything on the line for this, obviously." Patric pauses to take a very deep breath from the bottom of his lungs.

"I am sure there was a lot of debriefing and red tape going on with Webb and the FBI, but he will come out of this in top form. He has always been an honest and respected leader. He and his group are up against a powerful entity but their time is short.   With the new Presidential hopeful vowing to shut down Gitmo and with this financial crisis looming, their focus on a cover up on this must be low priority right now. Hopefully, that opens the door for Webb to get the information he needed and subsequently, validating my story."

"So your story is written? It's a little ballsy calling out members of the administration.   Are you sure you are ready for the ramifications?" Patric playing a bit of devil's advocate with his friend, but also knowing full well neither Tim nor the Times is going to print something prematurely, or lacking validity. "These bastards better not get away with this. America does not deserve this. They have already destroyed our reputation and respect in the world with their undocumented invasion and continuous war in Iraq...and now this."

"What does Bec know?" Tim is concerned for his friends, but the always the interrogative investigator.

"Very little. Drew didn't want to mention anything until all of the facts are in and the investigation is complete, especially where she became involved. He has a lot of guilt going on there." Defending Rebecca's father, Patric also wants to protect her from any more fear or pain.

"Drew? You and the old man are on a first name basis now? Things must be getting on pretty well. I do understand his feelings though. Can you imagine how he must feel. I'm sure he takes full responsibility for what happened." Being a new father puts things into a completely different perspective for Tim now. "Imagine if..."

"Don't even go there buddy, I know what you are thinking. Come on. We'd better get back in there. I don't want Bec getting any ideas about making babies. I'd prefer to just practice consummation for a while...a long while." Patric chuckles and they re-enter the room. The girls are chatting and laughing, probably telling old Tim and Patric stories as the baby sleeps soundly in Maureen's arms.

The television has been on in the background, though the star in the room, Timothy Patrick Connelly, has been stealing the show. It is an election year and of course the 24 hour cable news channels can't help but shove 24 hour campaign trail and poll images down the throats of whoever will watch. It seems that the Democratic hopeful candidate is speaking this afternoon and they all turn there attention to the screen. Tim picks up the remote to increase the volume.

The candidate speaks. *"If the United States has actionable intelligence that Osama bin Laden is hiding in Pakistan, I as President will commit US forces to kill him if the Pakistan government is unable or unwilling to take him out, then we have to act and we will take him out."*

Tim, Patric and Rebecca stand focused entirely on the television.

196

All three of them stand, glazed, their mouth's gaped wide open.

"That's impressive, especially when the current president says that he doesn't spend much time thinking about bin Laden anymore." Tim comments with a laugh and everyone joins in the laughter.

Patric gets close to Tim, and whispers in his ear. "What are the odds that is where he went from Cuba?" Tim nods and gives his friend a most serious glance as his cell phone begins to ring.

"Connelly here....Yes sir." Tim turns to Patric and mouth's the words, "It's Weller."

"We're still at the hospital." Tim's conversation with Bill Weller continues. "You are kidding me. Yes sir, I will. Thank you."

"What's up?" Noticing that whatever Bill Weller just told Tim was of major significance. Tim seems to be nearly in shock. The color has drained from his face and he appears to have checked out, staring off into the distance.

Tim turns back to Patric. "The frickin' television media are on their way to the Times building to interview me. Weller just said that Drew Webb fully validated the story along with high ranking FBI officials and it has been released. Worldwide my friend. Bill Weller wants us there, at the Times for the press conference." Filled with both pride and fear, Tim slowly lowers his arm, phone in hand.

"Not me Kemo Sabe. This is your story." Patric easily gives Tim full credit and totally releases himself from any further responsibility. "My job is finished here my friend." He puts his arm around Rebecca and pulls her close to him. "Are you ready? Let's give Mo some rest."

"What is going on you two? What story?" A very interested Rebecca looks at both of her friends over the edge of her nose, head lowered.

"Your father will be able to explain everything to you now, babe."

"Can I steal Patric away again for just a minute, Bec?" Tim points toward the door with his head.

"I don't know what you two are up to, but I can't help but trust you. Of course, go ahead. I will just have some more baby talk over here." Rebecca winks as she turns back to Maureen though she can tell both mother and baby are ready for a rest. Tim and Patric step outside the room and into the fluorescently lit hallway. With the door still ajar Tim stands very close to his friend as he begins to deliver just a few of the details of the story that has just been released. ***Wicked Game-The Hunt for bin Laden***, *by Timothy Connelly and Bill Weller, The New York Times.*

"We did imply that members of the administration have been holding bin Laden in Cuba for an unknown period of time, and that there intentions of releasing this information publicly was most definitely tied to the timing of the upcoming election. It won't be looked upon very well by voters who learn that the current administration, once again, had bin Laden by the balls and let him go, or get away, whatever the case may be." Tim confides in his friend and partner.

"Holy shit. That is outstanding. So, where the hell do you think he is?" Patric can't help but be excited for his long time pal and with some self pride for his own involvement in the materialization of this story. These two gentleman have done some extraordinary things together as a team, but these past six months have to be their most meaningful and finest, professionally as well as personally. Not withstanding a few, no less than hairy, moments, all seems to be falling into place for them now.

"Obviously, no one knows for sure, but if I were a betting man my friend, my money would be on Pakistan. He would have some level of protection there and being a quasi-ally of the United States, it would be hard for us to use military force to do much searching there. The Pakistanis will commit to cooperate with the US, but won't hand him over on a silver platter either. Once again politics gets in the way."

Tim continues, "I need you to come with me to the Times for these interviews. Don't wig on me now partner, I need you." Tim implores Patric as suddenly their roles have reversed, though now Patric's calling has been satisfied and Tim really doesn't need him anymore. For moral support and friendship perhaps, but not for this. For whatever divine reason they were serendipidously brought into this predicament of international intrigue, Patric is ready now to walk off into the sunset with his leading lady. No more adventure, and no credit due. Just the peace of having his girl safe and back in his life, though this time, he will not let her get away.

"This is your day Timbo. You've got your son, you've got your story. This is totally your day." Patric turns back into the room. Rebecca says her goodbyes to Maureen and walks toward Patric with the most amazing glow upon her face. He watches her approach as the sunlight from the window angelically illuminates her hair, he reaches out for her hand and pulls her close. They kiss.

"Good Luck." Patric shakes Tim's hand.

Rebecca kisses him on the check. "I think your family is ready for a nap. We'll see you guys soon."

As Patric and Rebecca make their exit, down the corridor a few members of the press are bursting their way toward family Connelly's room. Patric takes Rebecca's hand and they duck into a doorway to watch as the press continues past them.

"Tim, Tim Connelly, is it true that you broke this story?"

Tim comes out of the room, closing the door behind him protecting his wife and son to respond to their questions, "Well, I had a lot of help." He stands tall and dodging media heads, peaks down the hall at Rebecca and Patric who now turn and continue down the corridor, seemingly in slow motion, arms wrapped tightly around each other, off into the sunset...not looking back.

CHAPTER SEVENTEEN

TWO AND ONE HALF YEARS LATER...

THE ROOFTOP OF THE METROPOLITAN CLUB IS adorned in candlelight and flowers on this lovely spring evening in New York City. It is April 30th (2011) and the nuptials of the Honorable Drew Webb and his new bride Ms. Leslie March Webb have just concluded. It is a small but impressive gathering of Manhattan and Washington dignitaries, business people, family and friends. The lights of the city start coming up as the sun begins to set behind Central Park. The deep orange sun reflects from the buildings on the West Side across the Park providing a stunning back drop to this festive occasion. The patio terrace is transformed into an incredibly scenic dance floor as the finest jazz ensemble in the city plays softly from the north end of the patio. Drew Webb and his lovely new bride along with daughter Rebecca and her husband Patric Taylor mingle through the crowd greeting guests as tuxedo and white glove adorned waiters stroll through the crowd with trays of champagne and hors d'oeuvres.

This beautiful and historic building is such a fitting spot for the Webb nuptials. Founded in 1891 by a then very prominent group of gentlemen in the business and social communities of New York City and with JP Morgan as their first president, it is only fitting, being a member himself, that Drew Webb would choose this location. The club stands on the corner of Fifth Avenue and 60th Street, next to the Pierre Hotel and just across from Central Park South and the square at The Plaza.

The property was acquired in March of 1891 from the Duchess of Marlborough who signed the purchase agreement at the US Consulate in London. Cornelius Vanderbilt signed on behalf of the membership of the new club, and construction began. After three years and nearly $1.2 million dollars, which was quite impressive at the turn of the century, the clubhouse opened and hosted its first event in April 1894.

Rebecca Webb Taylor gives her husband a squeeze, "Isn't this wonderful? I am so elated to see Daddy so incredibly happy."

"Don't go getting all misty on me babe." He laughs. "Let's catch up with Tim and Mo." They shuffle away from Drew and Leslie and join their dear friends.

"Great day...great occasion." Tim holds up his glass.

"Yes Rebecca, I know you must be so thrilled for your father." Maureen adds to her husband's toast.

"Thank you both. We are really thrilled. I am so glad that he has found someone to share the rest of his life with. I know my mother is looking down from heaven very pleased."

The dining room inside the patio doors is being set for dinner and many of the guests are making their way inside to be seated. Totally unprompted, the band begins to play one of Rebecca's favorite classics, *My Funny Valentine*, and of course, being the ever hopeless romantic, Patric can't help but notice. "How about a dance with your husband before we go inside?" He extends his hand to his beautiful bride and sings in her ear. "Don't change a hair for me, not if you..."

"How can I resist that invitation? Come on you two, join us for a little dance before dinner?" Turning to Maureen and Tim, Rebecca takes Patric's hand and the four of them move toward the band, champagne still in hand. "Maureen, I don't think I've ever seen two hotter guys in tuxes than our dates this evening!" Rebecca's ivory silk gown reflects the little bit of sunlight that is left in the sky and takes on a beautiful pink hue. Her soft back totally exposed by the deep A-line cut of the back of the dress which comes together just above her tailbone.

Patric moves his hand tightly around Rebecca's bare back and pulls her so close they can literally feel each other's heart beating through their clothes as they sway to the beautiful music. "This is like a dream," she whispers softly into her husband's ear.

"Everything is complete now. Tim is a famed and respected journalist, not to mention he and Mo are great parents, we are where we've always been meant to be, and now my father is finally happy again." She looks around, taking in the city view. "God, I love New York."

They finish their dance and continue inside to join the rest of the guests for dinner. The room is tastefully appointed in white...white linen, white flowers, and white candles. The four dear friends make their way to the family table to be seated. Rebecca takes her seat beside her father and Patric, of course, next to his stunning wife. Somehow Tim and Patric have managed to be seated next to each other like two little boys at their first adult dinner party, rather than the traditional boy-girl seating. The room buzzes with the dull roar of conversation as the waiters begin to serve the dinner guests.

"How is Bec doing? Do you think she is finally over what happened?" Tim leans close to Patric, not wanting Rebecca to hear.

"She's doing great. I don't think she will ever forget what happened, it really shook her. But we don't really even talk about it much anymore. She's good." Patric looks at Rebecca with such a sense of pride and of course, deep adoring love. He has become more than her husband, but also a very important part of this family and very close to his father in law. Drew stands to make a toast as the room becomes very quiet, except for the quiet jazz dinner music coming from the patio terrace.

Holding his glass high, Drew speaks. "Friends, welcome. Thank you for being with us this evening." He looks down at his smiling bride. "To my beautiful wife, Leslie Webb. I can't thank you enough for not only agreeing to become my wife, but for all your love and support these past years. You are truly the light of my life and I look so forward to sharing the rest of my years with you." A loud "here-here" echos around the room, the ring of champagne glasses coming together in toast as Leslie stands with her husband.

The new husband and wife share a kiss and she remains standing at his side. He continues. "And to my daughter Rebecca and her husband Patric. I am so blessed to have such a wonderful daughter and fine son in my life. I love you both dearly."

Another "here-here" from the crowd as Rebecca and Patric toast the bride and groom and then turn to toast each other as they whisper, "I love you" to one another.

"Now, with no further adieu, please, enjoy your evening, and thank you all again for being with us here tonight for this wonderful celebration." Drew Webb raises his glass one more time to his guests and he and Leslie are seated.

Loving a great party, the guests dine, drink and dance the night away, into the wee hours atop the roof of the Metropolitan Club, on this lovely April night in the city.

As dawn approaches on this late April night, the stars fade and give way to the first day of May. A new dawn, a new day, one that will end an era.

* * * * *

CHAPTER EIGHTEEN

PAKISTAN MILITARY ACADEMY AT KAKUL, next to Abottabad, Pakistan, a tall dark man addresses a classroom of students in front of a black board, standing tall, hands folded in front of him. The man is of calm demeanor, exuding tactical intelligence as the students give full attention to their instructor.

The Kakul Academy, Pakistan's most prestigious of military schools, is located just one block from the compound where Osama bin Laden seems to have laid roots from Cuba. How did the al-Qaeda leader elude capture for nearly a decade during the prior administration and subsequent to the horrific events of September 11, 2001, only to be found living just one block from the Kakul Military Academy?

Though the Pakistan government claimed to have no idea that the al Qaeda mastermind lived, for what appears to be years, in this little town that conveniently also houses a large military base and only an hour from the capital city. It is somewhat hard to believe that this walled compound was constructed sometime after 2005 and relatively un-noticed in a small town with well groomed streets and home mostly to common military families and retired officers. The area is known for its good schools, some even established by Christian missionaries. Locals are said to have assumed the compound must have been that of drug dealers, never imagining it could be that of the most sought after terrorist leader of the past two decades.

FROM A REAL-TIME VIDEO FEED INTO THE WHITE HOUSE, the President and his advisors sit around a table watching "Operation Neptune Spear." In his speech, May 2, 2011, the president acknowledged that soon after taking office he instructed the director of the CIA to make the killing or capture of bin Laden the top priority and under his directive Operation Neptune Spear successfully took out the terrorist leader after 9 months of grueling strategic intelligence planning.

The raid in Pakistan was filmed by an RQ-170 Sentinel Drone and broadcast live to officials in the Situation Room where they watched the Navy SEALS carry out their mission. The Special Ops Forces would collect all evidence possible from the compound including computer equipment, flash drives, other storage devices and any other evidence that could provide information relative to the terrorist organizations' future plans.

Though the United States government offered the body to the Saudi Arabian government, since bin Laden was a Saudi citizen and member of a prominent Saudi family, their government declined and following strict Muslim code for burial, bin Laden was prepared for and ultimately buried at sea by the Special Ops Unit who carried out their mission, ending the era of Osama bin Laden.

THE PRESIDENT, Sunday, May 1, 2011

"Good evening. Tonight, I can report to the American people and to the world that the United States has conducted an operation that killed Osama bin Laden, the leader of al Qaeda, and a terrorist who's responsible for the murder of thousands of innocent men, women and children..."

* * * * *

This night was not only the end of the bin Laden era, but for three young friends, who personally experienced just a small part of this odyssey, closure could finally happen. For them along with so many other families in America and around the world who were affected by the events of 9-11 as well as countless other terror events involving this horrific terrorist leader.

For Rebecca and Patric Taylor, Maureen and Tim Connelly and Drew and Leslie Webb, an experience they will not soon forget, but now, finally, can have peace and resolution.

Author, Gerri Wilson divides her time between Hilton Head Island, South Carolina, the beautiful blue waters of the Bahamas and the crisp Colorado Rockies in the Vail Valley. In addition to writing, she is also an avid reader, sports enthusiast and Partner of Pinnacle SE Publishing (Pinnacle Self Edition Publishing) helping other authors to bring their manuscript ideas and works to reality.

www.wickedgameanovel.com